"I've come t[o] marry me[.]

"Marry you?" Nicole said faintly, unable to believe she could have heard him correctly.

"You sound astonished. Why?" Alex asked bluntly.

"Well...because...because I didn't think you were interested in marrying anyone...least of all me."

"Until recently I wasn't. As you may know, I was married once...a long time ago." His expression remained impassive. "But I've spent too long looking back. Now I have to look to the future. Your son needs a father. My father needs a grandson." Alex paused for a moment. "I think you and I both need the practical benefits of marriage. Companionship. Moral support. And someone to share our bed..."

**Anne Weale celebrates
her 75th novel for Harlequin® with
*Desert Honeymoon***

Dear Reader,

This story came into my mind during one of the happiest journeys in a lifetime of wonderful travels.

Several of my forbearers lived in India during the British Raj. As a child I listened to their reminiscences of a land that sounded far more colorful and exciting than England—where I grew up. Unwittingly, my great-uncles and great-aunts, who had gone abroad out of duty rather than inclination, sowed the seeds of my wanderlust.

I've been traveling the world since I was twenty-one. But somehow my destinations never included India. My son made that dream come true. Having arranged to canoe down India's most sacred river, the Ganges, he suggested that, afterward, his father and I should meet him in Delhi and he would take us to some of his favorite parts of the country.

The region I found most romantic was in the far northwest...the remote walled cities of Rajasthan. I hope this story will bring you some of the magic of Rajasthan.

Anne Weale

Books by Anne Weale

HARLEQUIN ROMANCE®
3474—A MARRIAGE HAS BEEN ARRANGED
3520—THE BARTERED BRIDE

Desert Honeymoon
Anne Weale

TORONTO • NEW YORK • LONDON
AMSTERDAM • PARIS • SYDNEY • HAMBURG
STOCKHOLM • ATHENS • TOKYO • MILAN • MADRID
PRAGUE • WARSAW • BUDAPEST • AUCKLAND

ISBN 0-373-03572-1

DESERT HONEYMOON

First North American Publication 1999.

Copyright © 1999 by Anne Weale.

This edition published by arrangement with Harlequin Books S.A.

® and TM are trademarks of the publisher. Trademarks indicated with
® are registered in the United States Patent and Trademark Office, the
Canadian Trade Marks Office and in other countries.

Visit us at www.romance.net

Printed in U.S.A.

CHAPTER ONE

ON HER way to the final interview, Nicole still didn't know whose advertisement she had answered, or how many others had survived the first weeding out. In fact she knew little more than she had after reading *The Times* advertisement offering a suitably qualified person an interesting and challenging post, at a generous salary, in an exotic location, its exact whereabouts unspecified.

That she had been short-listed was encouraging, but to be the winner of this strange contest was something else. Design was a crowded field. She knew she was a good designer, but she didn't underestimate the competition she would be facing.

The address to which she had been summoned was in the most fashionable part of London. It turned out to be an elegant block of flats with a uniformed hall porter in gold-buttoned pale grey livery. While Nicole gave him her name, she was aware of being scrutinised by a younger man in a business suit...a man who had 'plain clothes policeman' or 'ex-Special Air Service' written all over him.

She met his eyes, seeing in them not the smallest flicker of interest in her as a woman. Clearly he was a security guard of the most efficient kind. Any unauthorised person trying to get past him would be in big trouble. Which meant that the owners of the apartments must be very important or very rich: the kind of people who needed impregnable protection.

'You'll find Dr Strathallen in Flat Two on the fourth floor, madam,' said the porter, escorting her to the lift where he leaned in to press the button for her. As the door glided into place, shutting her inside the most luxurious elevator she had ever been in, Nicole considered this clue.

Was Dr Strathallen male or female? Was he or she the so far unidentified prospective employer? What kind of doctor was he or she? Not medical presumably. Why would a physician need the services of a textiles designer?

Before she had time to work out what kind of doctor might need such services, the lift opened at the fourth floor, revealing a carpeted corridor. Directly opposite the lift was an alcove containing a sofa and, above it, a painting Nicole recognised as a Gustav Klimt. Surely it couldn't be an original Klimt…could it? Perhaps at this level of living, even the pictures in the corridors had to be the genuine article.

At one side of the alcove, a discreet sign indicated the direction in which she would find the entrance to Flat Two. Her footsteps muffled by the carpet and its thick springy underlay, Nicole arrived there exactly on time and pressed the bell.

Within moments the door was opened. She found herself confronting a man whose grey eyes seemed even colder than those of the guard in the lobby.

She had never been shy or timid, even in her teens. But at first glance something about this man zapped her normal self-confidence. Perhaps because, without being in any way handsome, he was incredibly attractive. She had never met anyone, in real life, whose charisma struck her so forcibly. Some film stars had this sort of impact when they appeared on the screen, but ordinary men didn't, at least none she had ever met.

Conscious of a constriction in her throat, she said, 'Dr Strathallen?'

He nodded. 'Come in.' His voice was deep and brusque, giving the impression he had better things to do than interview her and was irked by the necessity of it.

As she obeyed his gesture and moved past him, Nicole was assailed by a powerful awareness of his physical presence; his height, his build, his aura of extreme fitness. In a totally inconsequential flashback, her memory transported her to a day in her childhood when her parents had taken her to the Regent's Park Zoo. She hadn't enjoyed it. The sight of wild animals in cages had upset her.

The one she remembered most clearly was the cheetah. The placard attached to its enclosure had said that, over short distances, it was the fastest animal on earth, hunting in daylight by sight rather than scent. She remembered reading that it was an endangered species, extinct in many of its former habitats. At the zoo, the size of its cage had permitted the creature only to pace its domain. It could never run at full speed, never enjoy its power.

Why the man now shutting the door should remind her of the captive cheetah was hard to fathom. But he did. Perhaps it had something to do with his tan. Here in London, at the end of an exceptionally wet summer, pallid faces were the norm and the tans acquired on beaches in southern Europe had soon faded when holidaymakers returned to their native climate.

But Dr Strathallen's lean features, as he gestured for her to precede him through an open door at the inner end of the hall, had the tan resulting from a naturally olive complexion being exposed to a hot climate for much longer than the longest vacation.

The large room where the interview was to take place was decorated and furnished with an elegance that married European taste with some fine things of Eastern origin. But precisely where in the vast Oriental world these artefacts came from she wasn't sure.

To her regret, she wasn't widely travelled. It was one of several reasons why she wanted the job. She longed to see more of the world. But that wasn't her principal reason for hoping that, despite his unfriendliness—he hadn't smiled or shaken hands—Dr Strathallen would prefer her to the other candidates.

'Sit down.' He indicated one of two sofas facing each other across a large low glass table.

'Thank you.' Nicole sat, placing her bag beside her on the cream-upholstered, feather-filled cushion into which she had sunk.

She was five feet six, but the sofa was designed for long-legged six-footers like the man relaxing opposite her. He was able to rest his broad shoulders against the back cushions whereas she had the choice of sitting upright or lounging which, in these circumstances, wasn't an option.

For what seemed a long time he looked at her in silence. Nicole forced herself to hold his gaze while longing to look away. There was something extremely disturbing about that silent surveillance even though, like the security man, he didn't send out the vibes of a virile man looking at a bedworthy woman. Not that bedworthy was the look she wished or tried to project.

Today she had dressed to look businesslike and efficient. Even so several men on the train and in the concourse of the mainline station had given her the eye. She knew, without vanity, that she was still attractive. At thirty-two, she hadn't yet lost the sex appeal inherited from her far more glamorous mother.

When it seemed he was never going to break the silence, she found herself asking, 'Have you many people to interview?'

'Five...all equally well qualified. The choice depends on my judgment of who is best suited to the demands of the environment. Would you like some coffee?'

'Yes, please.'

As he leaned forward to reach for a bell on the table between them and give it a vigorous shake, she couldn't help noticing the way his thick black hair sprang from a high broad forehead. Even if she hadn't known about his doctorate, the highest academic degree in any field of learning, even if he had been a stranger sitting opposite her in an Underground train, she would have guessed he was clever, possibly brilliant.

Appearances could be misleading but no one with a spark of intuition could fail to read the signs of a penetrating intelligence...or to pick up the indications that he might also be a demanding, even difficult leader in whatever field he excelled in. Uncompromising was the word that sprang to her mind. She wondered if she could cope with another dogmatic person in her life.

'What kind of environment is it?' she asked, eager to know what lay behind the somewhat cryptic reference to an exotic location.

He answered her with a question. 'How's your geography?'

'About average.'

'Do you know where Rajasthan is?'

'Of course…it's a state in the north of India,' Nicole said coolly. She had thought he was going to quiz her about somewhere far more obscure. Not that she was all that knowledgeable about India, but she had often browsed through Dan's atlas, wondering when, if ever, she might be able to satisfy her longing to see other countries, other cultures.

'What else do you know about it?'

'Not a lot. I know it has a famous desert.'

'The Great Thar Desert.'

Nicole knew how the name was spelt but, until he pronounced it, she hadn't known the 'h' was silent.

At that moment another man entered. He looked to be about fifty, with jet-black hair turning grey, a slight physique and thin hands. He was wearing European clothes but was recognisably Indian.

'Coffee, please, Jal,' said Strathallen.

With a slight bow the man withdrew.

'At the western edge of the desert,' Strathallen continued, 'there's an old walled city called Karangarh. How would you feel about living and working there?'

'If I hadn't been prepared to go more or less anywhere, I wouldn't have applied for the job,' Nicole replied.

'But from the questionnaire you filled in it appears that your travels so far have been limited to a few conventional tourist resorts in Europe?'

'Because I haven't had the time or the means to go further afield, not because I haven't wanted to,' she told him. 'After my mother's death, my father wanted me to share his holidays and I wanted to be with him while he was lonely without her. Now he's married again and has my stepmother to go on holidays with him. Which leaves me free to go wherever I please.'

This explanation wasn't untrue. It was a version of the truth that would give a better impression than the whole truth. Nicole felt the facts of her life, except those relating to the job she was applying for, were nothing to do with Dr Strathallen. Also he didn't strike her as a man who would have much understanding of the complexities and pressures affecting the lives of lesser mortals than himself.

The manservant returned with a tray. To have come back so soon he must have been expecting the request and had everything in readiness. Silence fell on the room while he went through a practised ritual of serving the visitor and then his employer—if in fact that was their relationship.

For reasons there wasn't time to define, Nicole sensed that Dr Strathallen wasn't the owner of this luxurious and sophisticated apartment. It didn't match his persona. Indeed the clothes he was wearing, a well-cut grey suit with a light blue shirt and dark blue tie, didn't quite 'go' with the general air of the man.

She had no idea what was worn by the inhabitants of the Great Thar Desert, if it had any. But she had read a book about the fierce Tuareg tribesmen of the Sahara. She could easily visualise Strathallen riding over a rolling sea of sand dunes, mounted on a camel, with a black turban on his head and an indigo 'veil' protecting his nose and mouth from the gritty desert wind while his narrowed grey eyes searched the empty horizon.

What it was about the man that caused her imagination to present her with this vivid improbable picture, she couldn't tell. Except that the body inside the businessman's clothes looked more powerful than that of any men she'd encountered, and his face was a tough man's face, not that of a number cruncher or anyone desk-bound.

The manservant withdrew, leaving them each with a poured cup of coffee, with a pot containing a couple of refills beside it. The cream jug and sugar bowl were near Nicole. She didn't take sugar but added some cream to her cup.

'Do you take these?' she asked, ready to pass them to him.

'No, thanks. I don't eat biscuits either,' he added, referring to the plate of English biscuits also left near her cup. Nicole had concluded that he didn't when a plate and a white-on-white embroidered napkin had been set out for her but not for him. Normally she enjoyed biscuits, but right now she didn't want to have her mouth full when he shot a question at her.

Normally calm and self-possessed as befitted her years, suddenly, in Dr Strathallen's presence, she felt her poise cracking as if she were an apprehensive twenty-year-old instead of a mature woman.

'How large a place is Karangarh?' she asked.

'A long time ago it was an important city ruled by a long line of princes. The palace at Karangarh is still owned and occupied by His Highness Prince Kesri, the Maharaja of Karangarh, who is also the owner of this apartment.'

Strathallen broke off to drink some coffee. Nicole found that, even with milk, hers was still too hot for her to take more than a sip.

'His life is completely different from that of his fore-bears,' he went on. 'A large part of the palace has been converted into a hotel. Another wing is a hospital.

Other buildings are workshops for craftsmen. The Maharaja was educated in England and America. He knows that eastern artefacts often need modifications to appeal to western tastes. That's why he wants a western-trained designer to oversee the export side of the business.'

'What sort of skills do his craftspeople have?' she asked.

'I'll show you part of a promotional video the Prince has had made.' He rose to go to a large cabinet made of some dark unfamiliar wood elaborately inlaid with silver and pieces of mother-of-pearl. He opened the doors, revealing a large television screen. After touching some switches he returned to his place on the other sofa, holding the remote control. 'This edited version was made to show the applicants for the post,' he told her. 'It only lasts seven minutes.'

Watching Nicole Dawson while her attention was concentrated on the screen, Alex was reminded of children's faces when they were listening to an enthralling story. Her expression showed the same rapt attention. Almost from the opening shot of the walled city of Karangarh rising out of the sandy wasteland surrounding it, she had become totally immersed in the colourful scenes being presented to her.

Already he had interviewed all but one of the other contenders and was becoming bored with the task entrusted to him. Designers were not on his wavelength, nor he on theirs. He disliked big cities and the kind of people who gravitated to them. Especially ambitious career women in designer suits with designer hair, diet-freak's bodies and complexions you could scrape off with a spoon.

Not that this woman was heavily made up or cat-walk-thin. Her figure couldn't be faulted and she had excellent legs. But she didn't flaunt them with a minuscule skirt and unnecessarily frequent crossings like two of the women at last night's dinner party.

London, New York and Paris—perhaps every capital city in the so-called 'civilised world'—seemed to be full of women who were either looking for a husband or a roll in the hay. He wasn't in the market for marriage, or for one night stands with the female equivalent of womanisers.

The nature of his life made sex a fairly rare indulgence. Women he found attractive were thin on the ground. Sometimes they weren't available, or weren't willing to accept his conditions: a cheerful goodbye when the time came to end the relationship

Looking at Ms Dawson, with her straight silky fair hair cut to curve into her neck just below the level of her determined-looking chin, and the soft sexy curves of her mouth, he felt a sudden strong urge to scoop her up from the sofa and carry her to his bedroom.

The thought of how she would respond if he acted on that desire amused him. Of course she would resist, vigorously. But would she really want to resist? Was the attraction mutual? Behind that cool façade, was she as red-blooded and as sex-starved as he was?

The questionnaire she had answered described her as unmarried, unpartnered, and with no family or other personal responsibilities which might interfere with her concentration on the job. Any woman of thirty-two, without a husband or a boyfriend, had to be sublimating.

Perhaps, for some women, it wasn't as hard as for most men. They seemed to vary a good deal in the strength of their libidos. Among those he'd known intimately, some had been disappointingly inhibited, others as ravenous as he was. It was hard to guess what Nicole Dawson might be like when, metaphorically speaking, she let her hair down.

When the video about Karangarh ended, it left Nicole with the feeling that, for a few minutes, a magic carpet had carried her to a fairytale world of sunlight, fabulous ancient architecture, and incredibly vibrant colours worn by women who walked like queens and men with black eyes and quick smiles.

'What a wonderful place!' she exclaimed. 'What's your work there, Dr Strathallen? Are you in charge of the hospital?' It crossed her mind that he might be in London for some medical conference and have been asked by the Prince to deputise for him in the choice of a designer.

He got up to switch off the TV and close the doors of the cabinet. 'The hospital is staffed by Indian doctors. I'm an anthropologist…studying Rajasthan's nomadic tribes. The Maharaja allows me to use the palace as my base.'

'Have you been out there long?'

He glanced at the watch on his lean wrist. She had already noticed the beautiful shape of his hands, with their long backs and longer fingers, the nails immaculately clean. 'We haven't much time, Ms Dawson. I need to know more about you. You'll find out more about me if you are selected to join the Prince's staff. He will decide who's appointed. He's already seen the preliminary reports. I shall email my reports to him tonight. You won't be kept waiting long.'

His snubbing reply to her question, which it

wouldn't have taken ten seconds for him to answer, and something in his demeanour made her certain he had already written her off. There was no rapport between them, no meeting of minds.

Which made it all the more annoying that she found him the most physically appealing man she had encountered since... Her mind shied away from the conclusion of that thought.

'What else do you want to know?' she said coldly, knowing that the interview had gone sour and she might as well go home now.

Nicole hadn't told her family she had applied for another job. They thought she was settled where she was. Rosemary, her stepmother, would have been horrified if she knew Nicole wanted to move, even in England, let alone abroad. There had been no point in upsetting Rosemary until such a move was definite.

How the rest of the family would react—would have reacted—Nicole wasn't sure. But it wasn't going to arise. She felt in her bones that Dr Strathallen had disliked her, that any day now a letter would come informing her that another applicant had been appointed.

When her stepmother called her to the telephone, saying that a Dr Strathallen wanted to speak to her, Nicole was astonished that he should take the trouble to break the bad news by phone.

She took the receiver from Rosemary. 'Nicole Dawson speaking.'

'Good evening, Ms Dawson.' His voice sounded even deeper and more resonant on the phone. 'The Prince has read my reports and feels that you and one other candidate are equally well-suited to the post. He would like me to talk to you both again. I suggest that this time we have lunch at a restaurant. Can you manage Friday?'

Luckily Nicole had some time off owing to her from her present employer because she had worked through two weekends on an important and urgent order.

'Friday would be fine,' she said.

'Good.' He gave her the name and address of the restaurant. 'We'll meet there at twelve-thirty?'

'I'll look forward to it.'

Strathallen didn't respond with the conventional 'So shall I'. Instead he said merely, 'Until Friday,' and rang off.

Nicole had scarcely had time to replace the receiver when Rosemary asked, 'Who is Dr Strathallen?'

The second Mrs Dawson never hesitated to ask personal questions or to intrude into other people's private lives. There was no way anyone living under the same roof with her *could* have a private life. She looked closely at every envelope that came through the letter box and had no compunction about reading other people's postcards.

'He's an anthropologist,' said Nicole. Knowing the next question would be 'Where did you meet him?' she was about to invent a white lie when her father intervened.

Mr Dawson, who was sitting by the fire, doing the crossword in his morning newspaper as he did every evening, looked up and said, 'Strathallen...anthropology...that rings a bell. Has he written a book on the subject?'

'I don't know, Dad. I know very little about him. He's looking for a designer and someone gave him my name.'

This was close to the truth but, she hoped, would

avoid a cross-examination by her stepmother. Fortunately it was almost time for Rosemary's favourite soap opera and her eagerness to learn the outcome of the dramatic climax at the end of the last instalment was stronger than her need to know about Nicole's telephone caller. As Rosemary picked up the remote control, Nicole, who wasn't a soap fan, said she had things to do upstairs.

'I'll say goodnight, Dad.' She went over to kiss him.

'Goodnight, my dear. Sleep well.'

She suspected he knew she found Rosemary a trial, although Nicole had never confided her problems to him. When Rosemary had entered their lives, Nicole had welcomed her, knowing that a man still in his early fifties needed more than a daughter's companionship.

It was only later, as Rosemary relaxed and allowed her true nature to show, that misgivings had set in. Her stepmother was not a bad woman, quite the reverse. It was her excessive goodness that was the problem. She wanted the best for everyone and put herself out to achieve it for them. But what she thought best wasn't always what they wanted.

Rosemary Dawson was a kind-hearted, well-intentioned control freak who refused to consider that her decisions and arrangements on behalf of her family, friends and acquaintances might sometimes be flawed or even completely disastrous.

'Goodnight, Rosemary.' Nicole managed to smile at her stepmother and forced herself to kiss the older woman's upturned cheek.

Inwardly, she was close to the end of her tether. Somehow she had to escape from the stifling atmosphere in this household. Her father, she knew, was resigned to it. He had married Rosemary during the long and desolate aftermath of his first wife's death. He would abide by that commitment, no matter how severely it taxed his patience.

Sometimes it seemed to Nicole that he was no longer the same person she remembered from her childhood. Something in him had died with her mother. Even with Dan, his grandson, he was not the same carefree, lively personality he had once been.

Dan had tackled his homework as soon as he came back from school. Now, in the small bedroom next to hers, he was sitting in front of his computer. 'Hi, Mum. Come and look at this.'

'It's almost logging-off time,' Nicole said, as she picked up a stool and placed it next to his chair.

'I know, but you must see this website. It's brilliant!'

She rested an arm on his shoulders and looked at the screen. What she really wanted to do was to hug him tightly to her. But although she still kissed him good-night, and Dan planted a kiss on her cheek before he got out of the car when she dropped him off at school, she took care not to be too demonstrative.

He was twelve now, on the verge of puberty when life started getting complicated...especially for a boy without a father. In looks, he took after her, with the same fair hair and hazel eyes. But the size of his hands and feet, and the way he was shooting up, indicated he was going to be a big man. It was her most fervent wish that, despite a bad start in life, he would also grow up to be a good man.

After taking her on a tour of the website, Dan closed down his PC and began getting ready for bed. At school, he was conscientious rather than clever. Team sports bored him. His overriding enthusiasm was for computers, an interest that Rosemary deplored but Nicole encouraged.

While he was in the bathroom, probably skimping his wash but giving his teeth a good brush because she had given him an electric toothbrush which kept going for two minutes, Nicole sat on the end of his bed. She wished she had had the luck, when her son was little, to meet a nice man who would have been a father to Dan and set him a good example. A grandfather wasn't the same. Her father did his best, but he couldn't do the things a man in his thirties would have done.

And it wasn't only for Dan's sake that she longed for a man in her life. She would have liked more children, a home of her own and someone to share her bed. From a personal perspective, her twenties had been as arid and empty as the Great Thar Desert. Now she was in her thirties and the few men she met were either married or had been through a painful divorce and weren't going to make another commitment in a hurry. She had long since given up hoping that a knight in shining armour was going to materialise and whisk her off to the life of her dreams.

That just wasn't going to happen. The only person who could make things better was herself, which was why she had answered the advertisement.

Walking from the Underground station nearest to her rendezvous with him, Nicole wondered what Dr Strathallen had written in his report on her. She now knew a bit more about him than she had at their first meeting.

Her father, who clipped newspaper articles on subjects that interested him, had unearthed a report of a lecture given by Dr Alexander Strathallen to the Royal

Geographical Society a couple of years earlier. His subject had been the Rabari nomads whose traditional way of life was under threat. Probably the only reason the talk had been reported was because he had made some controversial statements about the decline in moral values in the west.

Nicole had also found out from a girlfriend who knew about such things that the restaurant where he was giving her lunch was exceedingly fashionable and tables had to be booked long in advance. Not wanting to arrive first, when she came to the street where it was and saw that it was located close to the corner, she continued along the main road, window-shopping until her watch showed twenty-nine minutes past twelve.

The restaurant had a large plate glass window allowing passers-by to see the interior. As Nicole approached the entrance, she recognised Alexander Strathallen's hawk-like profile. He was seated on a sofa immediately inside the window and at right angles to it. But he wasn't alone.

There were two people with him, a man and a woman. The woman was leaning towards him from the opposite sofa, talking vivaciously and then breaking off to sip from a flute of champagne.

Dismayed at the thought of being interrogated by three people, Nicole raised her hand to open the door, but had it opened for her by a friendly young man who welcomed her to the restaurant. Then a smiling girl appeared to take her coat and umbrella. Although it hadn't rained so far, heavy showers were forecast for later. When, having handed over her things, Nicole turned towards Strathallen and his companions, she found he had already risen and was standing behind her.

'Good afternoon.' For the first time he smiled and offered his hand.

The smile transformed him from a somewhat forbidding personality into one of such charm that Nicole felt her insides do an involuntary flip. The feel of his long strong fingers closing over hers accentuated the reaction.

'Good afternoon.' She always shook hands firmly but now put all her strength into returning his clasp to avoid having her knuckles ground together. But his handshake wasn't the crushing grip she expected. Obviously he modified it when greeting women.

Then, instead of introducing her to the others, he said to the hovering young man, 'We'll go straight in and have our drinks at the table.'

Apart from one young couple so casually dressed that Nicole thought they had to be from the pop music world, or showbiz, the restaurant was empty.

'What would you like to drink?' her host asked, when they were seated.

Nicole's mind went totally blank. Perhaps it was the result of tension, followed by relief that the other people weren't with him, plus the jolt of attraction, but all the right answers deserted her.

'As we'll be drinking wine, let's stay with the grape, shall we?' Strathallen suggested. 'Two glasses of champagne, please.'

'Certainly, sir.'

When the young man had gone, Strathallen said, 'I arrived early and got into conversation with a couple of Americans. Nice people, but I didn't think you'd want to hear all the details of their itinerary. I hope coming to London again hasn't caused any problems with your present employer.'

'No, my working hours are fairly flexible. With all the people I've worked for since leaving college, I've always tried to give maximum input—never just the minimum required—and that's paid dividends. They've been understanding when I wanted to go on courses or take an extra day off.'

'What sort of courses have you been on?'

'Oh…time management…computer graphics skills…that kind of thing.'

The champagne arrived and with it two large folders containing the menus.

'To an enjoyable lunch,' said Strathallen, raising his glass to her before tasting the pale golden wine. 'Let's decide what to eat and then we can concentrate on other things.' He replaced the flute on the table and began to study the menu.

Nicole tried to match his concentration, but it was making a good second impression on the man beside her that mattered more to her than the specialities of a chef who, according to her friend, had already been awarded two Michelin stars and was said to be sure to gain the coveted third star before too long.

When the *maître d'hôtel* came to explain, in a pronounced French accent, some of the choices to her, she was conscious that, although he was very good-looking and charming, he didn't, for her, have the disturbing qualities of the darkly bronzed Scot beside her.

At least she presumed from his surname that Strathallen's roots were in Scotland even if, like so many of his countrymen, he chose to spend his life elsewhere.

After their food and wine had been ordered, on impulse she said, 'Does your wife like living in India, Dr Strathallen?'

As soon as the words were out of her mouth, she regretted them. There were no visible signs of his displeasure, but she couldn't have felt it more strongly if he had glared at her. Perhaps he expected her to let him lead the conversation. Or perhaps he didn't approve of being asked a personal question. For whatever reason, she sensed she had annoyed him.

'I'm not married,' he answered. And then: 'My way of life and domesticity don't mix. But why are you free of all attachments?'

The questionnaire she had filled in had required 'divorced' to be ticked if that was the applicant's status. So he knew she had never been married. But searching as it had been, the inquisition hadn't required her to state that she was a single parent. And she had no intention of revealing that fact to him now. Somehow she didn't think he would be sympathetic. He might even consider that Dan's existence disqualified her.

Some people wouldn't understand how a loving mother could contemplate leaving her child, even though, hopefully, it wouldn't be a long separation. Had Dan been younger, she wouldn't have left him. But at this point in his life, the potential benefits outweighed the drawbacks. She would miss being with him a lot more than he would miss her.

Reminding herself that she hadn't even got the job yet, and might never have it, Nicole said, 'I loved someone when I was younger. Unfortunately it didn't work out. Since then I've concentrated on my work. Perhaps I'll meet someone else someday...but I'm not holding my breath,' she tacked on lightly. 'There are other things in life.'

'Indeed there are—and food is one of them,' he added, as two more of the restaurant's staff arrived at their table, the one in the rear holding a large silver tray from which the other took a dish and placed it in front of Nicole.

She had chosen scallops as her first course. They came arranged in a circle surrounding a column of chicory. Earlier, a basket of long pointed brown rolls had been brought. As she broke hers in half and helped herself to butter, Nicole realised that she was hungrier than she had expected to be.

Usually, stress killed her appetite, and what could be more stressful than knowing that her future and Dan's depended on convincing Alexander Strathallen that she was the best person for the job?

CHAPTER TWO

FOR some minutes they ate in silence.

Strathallen had already finished his glass of champagne and started drinking the wine he had chosen to go with the meal. Nicole still had some champagne left and planned to go easy on the wine which, judging by her glimpse of the label when the wine waiter had displayed it, was several cuts above the plonk she drank on evenings with her friends.

She liked to relax with a glass of wine when she got home from work. But her father wasn't allowed to drink for health reasons and Rosemary was one of those non-drinkers who disapproved of alcohol as vehemently as reformed smokers disapprove of cigarettes.

She was the kind of woman who, if Nicole had kept wine in the sideboard in the dining room, would have watched to see how much she was drinking. So Nicole kept a bottle of supermarket plonk in a cupboard in her bedroom-cum-studio. The cupboard was locked because she knew Rosemary went in there while she was out. Keeping the bottle out of sight made her feel uncomfortable, but it was preferable to having Rosemary making critical remarks. She made enough of those as it was.

Closing her mind to thoughts of her stepmother, Nicole said, 'My father is interested in anthropology. He remembered a talk you gave to the Royal Geographical Society. Perhaps it wasn't reported accurately, but it gave the impression that you don't think much of the way the western world operates.'

He put down his knife and fork, leaned back in his chair and gave her the penetrating look that made her feel he could see inside her mind. 'I don't. Do you?'

'The west is the only culture I know.'

'You must have opinions about it.'

She had hoped to start him talking about his views, not to cause him to quiz her about hers. 'Of course...everyone has opinions, but they're not always worth expressing. Mine certainly wouldn't be worth a report in *The Times* as yours were.'

He shrugged. 'They were probably short of copy for that particular issue. But we didn't come here for me to expound my views. I want to know more about you. What do you do with yourself outside working hours?'

Most of Nicole's spare time was spent with her son, but she couldn't tell him that. She said, 'I walk...I read...I go swimming...I like to cook.' Though, since Rosemary's advent, her only chance to use the kitchen was when her father and stepmother went out to dinner with Rosemary's circle of friends.

'What sort of books do you read?' Strathallen asked.

'Anything and everything...mainly travel books and biographies.'

'No fiction?'

'Sometimes.' She wasn't going to tell him that, last thing at night, she often unwound in the pages of a romance. Men didn't read romances and tended to make fun of or despise them. They were not in touch with their emotions the way women were. Instead, she said, 'I rather like science fiction.' This was a taste she had acquired from Dan.

'Never tried it,' he said, a touch dismissively. 'But

when I'm out in the desert my choice of reading is dictated by space and weight considerations. I'll send you a list of books to read before you come to India. It's always a good idea to bone up on a place before one arrives.''

'Thank you—' It was a few seconds before the full impact of his statement sank in. When it did, her hazel eyes widened. 'Do you mean you're recommending me?' She couldn't conceal the surprise mingled with her delight.

'Unless you reveal some serious defect between now and the end of lunch...yes, I'm recommending you,' he confirmed.

Despite his amused reply, she sensed that he had some underlying reservation about his selection of her as the best of the candidates.

'How soon can you start?' he went on. 'How much notice must you give your present employers? I'm sorry...' The apology was tacked on because, in shifting his long legs under the table, his thigh had brushed against her knees.

Nicole knew the contact was accidental. He was not the type to play footsie. What disturbed her was her own reaction: an intense curiosity to know what it would be like to have this somewhat dour man make an amorous advance to her. Exciting...wildly exciting, was the next thought in her mind. And not only because he looked the way men were supposed to look— tall, lithe, with latent power and virility in every line of his body—but because there was also something primitive and untamed lurking under his seemingly civilised exterior.

She had felt it the first time they met when the memory of the caged cheetah had come into her mind. She felt it again now, so strongly that for a moment she couldn't collect her thoughts and answer his question.

Then she pulled herself together. ''Six weeks...is that all right?'

Walking back to his friend Kesri's apartment, a place the Prince seldom used himself but kept for the benefit of his aged great-aunts who belonged to an era when India's royal families had enjoyed every possible luxury, Alex wondered if in picking Nicole Dawson for the post he had made an error of judgment.

Her qualifications and those of the other finalist were evenly matched. He had selected Nicole for no better reason than that he wanted to see more of her...in every sense of the term.

He had found her attractive the first time he interviewed her, and today's lunch had heightened her allure. There was something elusive about her that appealed to the hunter in him. Women who were pushovers left him cold.

He remembered her explanation of why she was on her own. *I loved someone when I was younger. Unfortunately it didn't work out. Since then I've concentrated on my work.*

That, in essence, replicated his own situation. His job, and the places it took him to, precluded any close, long-term relationships. He was a loner and had been for a long time. As long as she understood that, and he'd already indicated the way things were with him, they could have a good time together. But like Kesri's liaisons, his own had to be without strings. There was no way he could share his life with a woman.

When Nicole told Dan about her new job, he said, 'Is it in London?' Then, his expression hopeful, 'Are we going to live there?'

Anxious to give him time to assimilate the change, she said, 'Would you like that?'

Dan nodded vigorously. 'It'd be great. I'd miss Granpa, of course, but I wouldn't miss *her!* Not having her breathing down our necks would be brilliant. That's one of the reasons I'm looking forward to being a boarder next term.'

It was the first time he had said in so many words that he didn't like his step-grandmother.

'No, it isn't in London. It's somewhere much further away...somewhere abroad,' Nicole told him.

Far from looking dismayed, he looked pleased. 'America?'

She shook her head, praying that what she said next wouldn't make him look crestfallen. 'Rajasthan...it's in India.'

For a moment or two he looked startled. Then his eyes sparkled with excitement. 'You're not kidding me, are you? Wow, that's brilliant, Mum.' A flicker of doubt subdued his initial enthusiasm. 'It's a long way. Won't the air fares be way too expensive for me to come for the holidays?'

'On what I'm going to be earning that won't be a problem. But it does mean we won't see each other except in the long holidays. I can't come back for your half-term and weekend leaves.'

'We can email each other every day. But, Mum, will *you* be all right...in India all by yourself?'

His concern made her smile, but there was a lump in her throat. 'You needn't worry about me. I'll be living in a palace.'

She began to tell him everything she knew about the

Prince and the picturesque walled city on the fringe of the desert.

Soon after Dan was born, her father had taken steps to ensure that his grandson could be educated at the independent school where he and his father and grandfather had been pupils. It was a family tradition that, in some ways, Nicole would have liked to break. In her heart she wasn't in favour of boys being sent away from home at the tender age of thirteen.

But Marsden wasn't one of England's famous public schools like Eton or Gordonstoun. It was a more modest establishment not far from where they lived. Also, not only had her father denied himself many pleasures to fund Dan's education, Rosemary's advent had changed Nicole's view of the situation.

There was another factor to consider. The local state school had been going downhill under a lax head teacher. It had a reputation for disorderly behaviour and poor exam results. The principal of her father's old school was a man of forceful character, with teenagers of his own. She felt Dan would be safer under his aegis than at the local day school with its overcrowded classrooms and lack of playground supervision.

Relieved to have her son's backing, Nicole went down to break the news to her father and stepmother.

Predictably, Rosemary was outraged. 'How can you even contemplate leaving your poor little boy?' she expostulated. 'It's bad enough that he doesn't have a father. For his mother to desert him—'

Keeping control of her temper, Nicole said quietly, 'I'm not deserting him, Rosemary. It will only be for a short time. At the end of term, Dan can fly out to join me.'

To her relief, before Rosemary could resume her de-

nunciation, Mr Dawson said firmly, 'If you hadn't
taken the initiative, I was going to suggest that, with
Dan away at school, it was time to broaden your ho-
rizons. You're doing the right thing, my dear. For almost thirteen years you've adapted your life to Dan's
needs and that was right and proper. Now it's time to
consider your own needs...time to spread your wings.
I can't think of anywhere more exciting to do that than
India.'

And then, to the surprise of both women, he directed
a quelling glance at his wife and said with great firm-
ness, 'Nicole has made a decision which I think will
benefit her and the boy. If you don't agree, Rosemary,
please keep your views to yourself.'

Nicole's night-flight to Delhi landed early in the morning.

When she emerged from the airport building, pulling
her suitcase behind her, a daunting scene greeted her.
What seemed like hundreds of people were waiting to
pounce on the passengers, grab their luggage and con-
vey them to their final destination.

In her jet-lagged state she was strongly tempted to
turn tail and go back inside the airport, especially as
none of the placards with European names on them that
were being brandished by some of the men behind the
barricades had her name written on it.

Reluctantly making her way to the opening in the
barrier through which other newly arrived foreigners
were passing ahead of her, she braced herself to hang
on to her luggage until whoever was meeting her materialised.

Then, with profound relief, she saw a familiar figure

making his way towards her. She was so glad to see him, her face lit up with delight.

Towering over the crowd, Alex Strathallen was also noticeable for his air of complete relaxation in a situation fraught with the tension of too many porters and drivers competing for too few customers.

While everyone else was shoving and pushing, he moved through the crush with the ease of a tall and commanding figure to whom smaller, less assured people automatically gave way. But his expression, she noticed, was not the chilly hauteur to be seen in old sepia photographs of the British who had run India during the Raj. He was smiling as he moved through the press, exchanging friendly words with those who let him pass.

'A bit of a madhouse, isn't it?' he said, when he reached her.

'A bit,' she agreed, with a smile. 'I'm glad I have someone meeting me.'

'Let's get you out of this maelstrom. Our driver will take your case—' he indicated an Indian who had come through the crush behind him '—and I'll take your backpack.'

He slipped the straps from her shoulders rather in the manner of a grown-up divesting a small child of its coat. Then, with it slung by one strap over his own broader, more powerful shoulder, he led the way through the multitude who now made no further attempts to impose themselves on her.

A few moments later she was in the back of a taxi and Alex was folding his long legs to fit the space beside her.

'How was the flight? Did you get any sleep?' he asked.

'Not a lot...but otherwise it was great. I enjoyed it. Very nice food...two good movies.'

'Who did you have sitting next to you?'

'An elderly couple celebrating their golden wedding with a trip to see the Taj Mahal.'

Perhaps it was only her imagination, but it seemed to her that, for a moment, something strange happened...like a shutter coming down. He was sitting beside her, but his mind was somewhere else.

She wasn't sure why, but his silence made her uneasy. After some moments, she asked, 'How are we getting to Karangarh? By train?'

'By air...but not till tomorrow. I have some business in Delhi and you need to break your journey. We'll fly to Karangarh after breakfast. Tonight we're staying at the Imperial, an oasis of calm right in the centre of Delhi.'

There were placid-looking pale grey cattle standing about, unattended, on the verges of the wide tree-lined road to the city. Near a roundabout where there seemed to be a hair-raisingly casual attitude to traffic lanes, Nicole noticed a slogan pasted on a hoarding. *Be not anxious about what you have, but about what you are.*

It reminded her of Rosemary's bitter disapproval of this undertaking. Her stepmother had been careful not to express it again in her husband's presence, but had found several opportunities to upbraid Nicole in private.

Am I being selfish? she wondered, for the umpteenth time. Saying goodbye to Dan had been agony. She could still feel his arms round her neck as they exchanged their last hug at the London airport where, with her father, he had seen her off.

If there had been tears in his eyes when they drew

apart, she didn't think she could have left him. But Dan, already keenly looking forward to his own flight to India in twelve weeks' time, had been cheerful rather than dejected.

She had had to seem cheerful too. Only in the privacy of a cubicle in the washroom on the airside of the security and customs barriers had she cried, but only briefly. Then she had washed her face, braced herself and joined the rest of the passengers waiting for flights to places even more distant than where she was going.

Beside her, Strathallen said, 'You'll feel better when you've had a bath. Then, if I were you, I'd go to bed until lunchtime. If you didn't nap on the plane, there's no way you can stay awake until bedtime tonight.'

'Whatever you say. You're the expert. How many times have you flown from Europe to India?'

'I've lost count. I've been coming here a long time. For me the culture shock is at that end, not this.'

Nicole's first impression of Delhi was of chaotic traffic and swarms of people. Then their taxi turned through a gateway where a short avenue of tall palms led to the porticoed entrance to a building.

The rear passenger door was opened for her by a massively built bearded and turbanned doorman. 'Good morning, madam.'

'Good morning. Thank you.'

When Strathallen came round the back of the taxi and took hold of her arm to escort her up the steps, it was the polite gesture of a man who at some stage of his life had been trained in traditional courtesies. But all the way up the entrance stairs and through the imposing lobby to the lift, she was conscious of the light touch of his fingers just above her elbow.

'Shouldn't I register?' she asked, at the door of the lift.

He released his hold. 'They can take your passport details later.''

'But the room key...'

'The door will be open.'

From the lift they entered a wide corridor decorated and thickly carpeted in a soft shade of apple-green. At the far end she saw her luggage being wheeled through a door by one of the hotel staff.

Moments later, to her surprise, she found the room he had entered was not her bedroom but an ante-room leading into a large and elegantly appointed sitting room.

'This is Prince Kesri's suite,' Strathallen explained. 'The hotel is full tonight. There's a large wedding party staying here.'

The luggage porter reappeared through the door of an adjoining room. He smiled and bowed to Nicole. Strathallen gave him a tip and was handed the room key.

When the man had gone, he said, 'Would you like some coffee or tea before you have your shower?'

'What I'd really like is some water.'

'It's in here.' Showing her that what she would have taken for an elegant sideboard was actually a luxury version of a mini-bar with glasses in one section and an ice-box in the other, he put some ice in a tall glass and opened the seal on a bottle of water with an effortless turn of his strong wrist. 'If there's anything else you need, call Room Service or Reception. The switchboard operator will give you a wake-up call if you want one. I'll be back about one. We'll have lunch in the garden. See you later.'

As he strode to the door, Nicole said, 'Thank you for meeting me. I hope it wasn't too inconvenient.'

As he opened the door, he turned. 'Not inconvenient at all. It was a pleasure.' He gave her one of his rare and charming smiles.

She was woken, as she had requested, at half past twelve. For some minutes she lay taking in the unaccustomed opulence of her surroundings. This bedroom was many times larger than her room in her father's house, with a lofty ceiling from which hung a large electric fan.

She had already unpacked fresh underwear and a change of clothes more suitable for lunch in a grand hotel than the combat trousers, shirt and zip-up fleece she had travelled in.

When she had dressed and put on a little light makeup, she went back to the sitting room to drink another glass of water. It was only then that she noticed there was another door opposite the entrance to the bedroom. Perhaps it was another bedroom for the use of the Prince's wife if he had one. So far she knew very little about her employer, although his forebears were mentioned in more than one of the books on the reading list she had received from Strathallen.

Curious to see what lay behind the closed door, Nicole opened it. As she had surmised, the room within was another bedroom—and someone was using it. There was a laptop computer with a couple of floppy disks on top of it on the writing table. A book with a marker protruding from it lay on the night-table between the twin beds. A document case had been left on one of seat cushions of the sofa facing the beds.

As she took in these indications that the room was

occupied and realised they had to mean that Strathallen was sharing the suite with her, Nicole remembered him saying the hotel was full. Even so, it seemed odd, to say the least, for him to have taken for granted that she wouldn't mind this arrangement. Surely the proper thing to have done was to book himself, or her, into another hotel?

Within a couple of minutes of her closing the door of his room, Strathallen joined her.

'Did you get some sleep?' he asked.

'Yes, thank you. I feel much better.'

'Good...then we'll go down and eat. No need to bring your key. I picked mine up from the desk in case you were still in bed.'

As they were walking to the lift, Nicole said, 'Won't the hotel staff think it strange...our sharing the Prince's suite?'

He looked down at her. 'Is that an oblique way of saying you don't want to share the suite with me?'

'I didn't say that,' she began.

'Women often don't say what they mean,' he said dryly. 'It's one of their characteristics. Taking your question at its face value, the hotel staff are paid to think about making us as comfortable as possible. What we do, unless it interferes with the comfort of other guests, isn't their concern.'

The lift was at another floor. He pressed the call button. 'Do you want me to move somewhere else?'

'No...no, of course not.' She could see that, from his point of view, it would be less convenient, not to mention more expensive. Presumably the Prince, not the sardonic-eyed man beside her, would be paying the bill for their stay here.

The lift opened. As she stepped inside, Nicole felt

herself blushing. She wished she had held her tongue. All she had done, by raising the matter, was to embarrass herself.

The hotel's garden was screened by tall trees that muted the noise of the city surrounding this exclusive oasis. Immediately outside the building there was a paved terrace where people were eating light refreshments. Beyond it was a sunlit lawn where tables were laid more formally.

A portly major-domo in leg-hugging white trousers, the knee-length tunic which she knew was called an *Achkan* and a spectacular crested green turban to match the broad sash round his middle came to meet them as they stepped onto the lawn.

'Dr Strathallen...*madame*...where would you like to sit?'

'In the shade, please. My guest arrived from Europe this morning. She might find the sun too hot.'

The major-domo conducted them to a table under a sunbrella. A waiter was summoned, gin and tonics brought.

'Does the Prince spend a lot of time in Delhi?' she asked.

'He comes about once a month. His sister works here. She's a gynaecologist and very involved in women's pressure groups. The Prince also tries to influence the future of India. He also enjoys the more sophisticated social life here...something that I would pay to avoid,' he added dryly.

'But surely everyone needs some social life.'

'I enjoy meeting my friends. I don't care for large smart parties.'

He had been looking at her, but now he turned his cool grey gaze on two groups of people taking their places at nearby tables. One was a party of well-dressed businessmen. The other group consisted of three attractive young women, one wearing European clothes, the second a silk sari and the third dressed in loose trousers and a long tunic, both garments made of pale blue and white cotton voile.

'What's the name of the outfit the girl in blue is wearing?' Nicole asked.

Strathallen had given them only cursory attention before turning back to Nicole. He must be exceptionally observant, she realised, when, without a second look at the three women's table, he said, 'That's a *salwar kameez*, traditionally from the Punjab, but city girls aren't sticklers for tradition. They wear what they like.'

At that moment Nicole caught sight of a small bushy-tailed striped creature darting across the grass towards the damask-clothed table on which, shaded by an awning, an array of puddings and gateaux awaited the lunchers after they had eaten their selections from the range of hot food in the huge silver-topped dishes on the main table.

'What's that little animal?' she exclaimed.

'A palm squirrel. They're the reason the puddings are protected by plastic domes. If they weren't, those little marauders would be tucking in with great gusto,' he said, smiling.

Perhaps it was just as well that he didn't smile often, she thought. Every time he did, it had a peculiar effect on the pit of her stomach.

He rose. 'Let's go and choose something to eat, shall we?' he suggested.

When lunch was over, Nicole expected him to leave her to her own devices for the afternoon. But he said,

'I have an hour to spare before my meeting. Do you feel like stretching your legs?'

The truthful answer would have been that she felt so full of delicious food that, on her own, she would have retired to her room for another nap. Instead she nodded and reached for her bag.

Leaving the grounds of the hotel was like entering another world, but only a short walk along the dusty, noisy main thoroughfare that Strathallen said was called Janpath was a relatively quiet sidestreet where women were selling textiles in all the roseate colours of dawn and sunset. Their wares were spread on a bank at one side of the lane like a huge magic carpet. On lines strung between the trees, hand-stitched quilts made from pieces of antique velvet and silk were displayed.

Although the vendors' cotton saris probably cost nothing compared with the silk ones worn by guests at the Imperial, the colours were still wonderful, perhaps enhanced by long exposure to the sun and many washings.

'How graceful they are,' she remarked to Strathallen.

'Grace seems to go with bare feet or flat sandals and to disappear with high heels.' He glanced down at her low-heeled shoes. 'I'm glad to see you don't wear them.'

She found some of his views irritatingly arbitrary. 'I do sometimes, when I'm not going to have to walk far.'

'I'll take you along to the government-sponsored emporium and leave you there,' said Strathallen. 'You'll probably want to spend an hour looking round the various craft sections and it's only a short walk back to the hotel. We'll convene for dinner about seven.'

*   *   *

Nicole was ready and waiting in the suite's sitting room when, a few minutes to the hour, Strathallen came out of his bedroom. His hair still damp from the shower, he was no longer wearing a lounge suit but had changed into chinos and a cotton shirt a little darker than his tan.

'You got back all right then?' he said.

'No problem,' she smiled. 'After I'd left the emporium I had a browse in a bookshop where the proprietor told me I must read this.' She held up the book she had bought.

Strathallen read out the title. *'A Princess Remembers...The Memoirs of the Maharani of Jaipur.* It's very popular with women tourists. The Maharani and her mother were both famous beauties in their day. I haven't read it myself but I'm told it's an interesting insight into a vanished era.'

'Why haven't you read it? Because it's written by a woman?'

His mouth curled with amusement. 'You think I'm a woman-hater?'

'Not a hater, that's too extreme, but perhaps not very pro women.'

'Not en masse,' he agreed. 'But there are some women whose company I enjoy. Don't tell me that, given the option of being, let's say, stranded somewhere with a group of men or women, you wouldn't choose your own sex as more likely to be on your wavelength.'

'That would depend on the situation. On a bus that had broken down in the middle of nowhere, I certainly wouldn't be the one to get it going and nor would most women. In any random group of men, there's almost certain to be one with mechanical know-how. I'm sure you would have a crack at fixing an engine. I wouldn't know where to begin.'

'I'd start by looking for the manual. Let's go down to the bar, shall we?'

As they left the suite, four women emerged from a door at the far end of the corridor. All were dressed in exquisite saris with borders of real gold thread. They glittered with costly jewels. But while three had their lustrous black hair uncovered, the fourth had her hair and face concealed by the shimmering folds of a diaphanous scarlet sari with gold embroidery all over it.

Like a cluster of iridescent dragonflies, they approached the lift.

'We'll go down by the stairs,' said Strathallen. Lowering his voice, he added, 'The one in red is the bride.'

As the three unveiled woman glanced at him, he placed his palms together and inclined his head in a gesture that made Nicole wonder if, behind the rather ruthless exterior he presented, there was a streak of chivalry.

CHAPTER THREE

'WILL her bridegroom have been chosen by her parents?' Nicole asked, as they walked down the staircase.

'Yes...and she probably has as good a chance of being happy as a western bride,' he said. 'Most of the people here believe that love is something that grows in a lifetime of living together.'

'Perhaps they're right,' said Nicole. 'I suppose if you grow up with the idea of your parents picking out a husband for you, it doesn't seem as outlandish as it does to us. Anyway our system isn't all that successful. But it must make their wedding nights horribly fraught if the brides and grooms barely know each other.'

'It may make them more exciting,' he commented dryly. 'It's no big deal going on a honeymoon with someone you've been sleeping with for months.'

'I should think it would be a much better deal,' said Nicole.

'Was your first time a disappointment?'

She couldn't believe he had asked such a personal question on so short an acquaintance. Her cheeks flaming, she said stiffly, 'I was speaking generally, not personally.'

He made no comment. She knew he didn't believe her. What made it all the more annoying was that his guess was correct. It had been the worst disappointment of her life. She had thought that love was the passport to rapture. Perhaps, for some people, it was. But it hadn't been for her.

When they reached the lobby, the bride and her attendants had just emerged from the lift and were moving in the direction of a wide corridor leading off the lobby.

'The hotel has a small shopping arcade,' said Strathallen. 'The windows might interest you. What did you think of the emporium?'

Still annoyed by his earlier question, Nicole said, with forced politeness, 'It was fascinating…a very useful overview of the things being made here. Thank you for thinking of it.'

'I'm glad you enjoyed it. Did you buy anything?'

'I was tempted several times, especially by the cashmere shawls, but I managed to resist them. It's usually a mistake to shop when you've just arrived somewhere.'

They had come to the first of the window displays he had mentioned. It was full of jewellery and ornaments of the type to appeal to wealthy tourists in search of lavish mementoes. Her taste ran to simpler things. She could see at a glance there was little she liked.

Again, Strathallen showed uncanny perspicacity. 'Not your style?' he asked.

'Not really…and I'm sure you would rather be sitting down with a drink. Was your meeting successful?'

'I don't know. I was summoned to address a government committee on ways to protect the interests of the nomads. Whether the committee was persuaded by my arguments only time will tell. Did you go anywhere else apart from the bookshop?'

'No, I came back and had my first taste of *lassi* on the terrace.'

She did not tell him she had also asked at the desk if the hotel had facilities for sending an email to Dan.

They had and, to her delight, when she had keyed in the password to her Yahoo mail box, there had been a message from him, sent the night before when he got home from the airport.

Dear Mum, Hope you enjoyed the flight. Did you have your own TV screen? Email soon. Lots of love. Dan xxx

Her reply had been longer. When he printed it out it would cover a couple of pages. She had included messages to her father and Rosemary. Once a week she would send an email for family consumption. The daily messages would be for Dan's eyes only.

'Did you like it?' Strathallen asked.

'What...? Oh, the *lassi*...yes, delicious. When the waiter told me it was made with yogurt, I was sure I would like it. I eat a lot of yog as—' She stopped short, on the brink of saying 'as my son calls it'.

Fortunately the bar steward was approaching the corner table where they had just sat down and his arrival distracted Strathallen's attention from her slight slip of the tongue.

In fact Alex was aware that she had clipped off the end of her remark. He also knew that, for a minute before that, her mind had been miles away from where they were.

He ordered a Golden Pheasant beer for himself and, at her request, a soft drink for Nicole.

When the steward had gone, he said, 'Yogurt is usually called curd here. When I'm at the palace I have it for breakfast with a banana and some of the local millet bread.'

She asked what he ate in the desert. As her interest seemed genuine, he told her. As he talked he was thinking about her reaction to his question on the staircase. It wasn't his habit to quiz women he had only recently met about their sex lives, but the question had slipped out. Clearly she had been startled and embarrassed. Which in itself told him a lot about her. Generally women of her age could take almost anything in their stride.

Perhaps all her sexual experiences had been unsatisfactory. Maybe that passionate mouth was misleading and she had emotional hang-ups which prevented her from enjoying making love. Or maybe she had picked the wrong partners. Some women made a habit of falling for men who wouldn't make them happy in or out of bed.

He found himself wishing that, instead of having a meal neither of them really needed after eating a substantial lunch, he could take her back up to the suite and make slow painstaking love to her.

The rose-coloured blush that had suffused her face on the stairs had been a powerful turn-on. He couldn't remember the last time he'd seen a woman blush. They didn't do it any more. In his father's youth, men had modified their language in mixed company. Alex himself had been raised not to swear in front of his mother and sisters. Even now, from long-ingrained habit, he still didn't use certain words when women were present. But, except in front of their parents, his sisters and their girlfriends all swore like troopers. They had also, before they were married, had enthusiastic sex with whomever they fancied. Why not? was their attitude.

He couldn't believe that, despite the blush, Nicole was any less experienced than most of her contemporaries. But going to bed with men and having a great time there were not necessarily concomitant.

He looked at the woman beside him with her slender yet ultra-feminine body and he wanted to give her pleasure...the pleasure she might have missed in her past relationships.

When Strathallen suggested they have a light supper in the hotel's Garden Room rather than in the main restaurant, Nicole was relieved. Now, by her body clock, it was past midnight. She wasn't tired, but nor was she hungry.

Neither was he, it seemed. After they had looked at the menu, he ordered chicken sandwiches and a bottle of white wine. When they had finished the sandwiches, he persuaded her to share a dessert called Banana Bonanza with him.

There was something curiously intimate about two people dipping their spoons into the same pudding, thought Nicole, making her spoonfuls last as long as possible so that most of the calories would be burned up in his big frame rather than hers.

The occupants of the surrounding tables probably thought they were on far closer terms than was actually the case. They might even think they were husband and wife, or lovers travelling together.

The thought of being in a close relationship with Strathallen—he had called her Nicole several times but she hadn't yet used his first name—started a tremor inside her. His ability to stir up feelings she would rather stay dormant annoyed her.

That side of her nature had brought her nothing but unhappiness and frustration. After the last disaster, she had made up her mind to stay celibate. Even though she had never actually experienced it with someone else, she knew she was capable of reaching orgasm. She had just never met a man who understood how a woman's body worked.

Why should Strathallen be different from the others? Not that the entire male sex could be judged by the three she had been involved with. But from everything she had read in women's magazines and agony columns, there were more inept lovers than brilliant ones.

The man across the table had all the physical qualifications. The attractive face. The great body. But how much did he know about women's bodies and their much slower, more complex responses?

There was still some wine in the bottle when he asked for their bill and signed the chit. 'We'll finish the wine in our room,' he told the waiter, as he gave him a tip.

Nicole expected the waiter to remove the bottle from the ice bucket, wipe away the condensation and wrap it in a napkin before handing it to Strathallen. But it remained on the table as they rose and left the Garden Room.

Hardly had Strathallen closed the outer door of the suite behind him than there was a knock from outside. He re-opened it to admit another waiter bearing both bottle and bucket and a tray with two glasses.

As the man set it down on the coffee table, pocketed a tip and departed, Nicole wondered if the sensible thing to do was to plead tiredness and say goodnight now.

If she stayed to share the rest of the wine, would it give a false impression? Or was she assuming, wrongly, that because she was intensely conscious of Strathallen's masculine magnetism, he was equally aware that she was a passable woman who might be willing if he were to try his luck? If he was that sort of man...and most of them were.

'What you have to realise is that India's greatest resource is people,' he said, filling the glasses. 'In the west, all forms of service are expensive. Do-it-yourself has become part of the culture. Here service is cheap. By using it, you're contributing to the country's economy. In human terms, everything you pay to have done for you is helping to give someone a slightly better quality of life.'

Nicole found it unnerving that he was so closely attuned to her thought processes that, yet again, he had known what was in her mind.

Bringing the glasses to where she was standing, he handed one to her. 'Some newcomers find it hard to adapt to that concept, but I don't think you will.'

'What makes you say that?'

'You're a woman. There are always exceptions to every generalisation, but on the whole your sex tends to be more sensitive and responsive to cultural differences.' He touched the side of his glass to the side of hers. 'Here's to your enjoyment of ''the Indian experience'' as the travel operators call it.'

'Thank you...and thank you for making my arrival so pleasant,' she added.

'Let's sit down.' He gestured at the sofa.

Nicole sat down at one end of it, hoping he would take the other. He didn't. He sat in the middle, crossing his long legs and swivelling his body towards her, resting one arm across the sofa's low backrest, his other hand holding his glass.

He appeared to be totally relaxed. Nicole had never been more tense. She was almost certain that, when he judged the moment was right, he was going to put his glass on the table and his other hand would come snaking along the backrest to draw her into his arms.

Her problem was that common sense told her it would be crazy to let him get away with it, but all the rest of her senses were voting the other way. She was consumed with longing to be held close to that hard chest and kissed by those firm male lips. Overwhelming attraction was not an emotion she was accustomed to dealing with. Instinctively she distrusted it.

To postpone the moment of decision—if her instinct was right—she said, 'I still can't believe I'm here. It all feels slightly unreal.'

He drank some wine. 'That's an effect of jet lag. It will feel more real tomorrow when your body clock has begun to adjust.'

Then, so casually and unhurriedly that it took her by surprise, he removed the glass from her hand and set it on the table with his own.

'I've been wanting to kiss you all evening,' he told her. And did.

Forewarned was not forearmed, Nicole discovered. She had been braced for this to happen, yet his mouth was on hers before she could do a thing to prevent it. And the instant their lips met, she didn't want to.

It was not a tentative kiss. It took her response for granted without going too far too fast. He gave her time to adjust to an unfamiliar embrace before tightening the arm round her waist and moving his other hand upwards till it reached the nape of her neck.

Knowing it was now or never, she mustered enough self-control to flatten her palms on his chest and push him away. 'Dr Strathallen...please...this isn't a good idea.'

Without releasing his hold, he allowed her to fend him off. To her astonishment, he laughed. 'You can't call a man you've been kissing by his surname. Try Alex. It won't commit you to anything you don't want,' he added, his grey eyes mocking her formality, but with a warmth it was very hard to resist.

'I definitely don't want this,' she told him firmly, wishing she meant it.

'I think you do...we both do...but I'm not going to pressure you.' He let her go, leaning back against the cushions and watching her with a combination of un-disguised desire and amusement. 'We're both old enough to know what we're doing. We want each other. Why pretend otherwise?'

'We hardly know each other.'

'OK, if that's how you feel, I'd better say goodnight. Just one more kiss and then to my solitary bed.'

With the same disconcerting swiftness that had caught her off guard before, he took her chin in his hand and brushed three feather-light kisses on her lips, the tip of her nose and her forehead. 'Sleep well...if you can sleep. Finish the wine. That might help.'

He rose and walked to his door where he turned to say, 'We need to breakfast at seven so you'd better fix a wake-up call. Goodnight.'

Nicole didn't linger in the sitting room after he closed his door. She put the bottle in the ice box, turned out the lights by the switches next to her door and, leaving his glass on the table, took hers into her room.

She was both relieved and disappointed. She couldn't fault the way he had handled her rejection, but felt that a nicer man wouldn't have made a pass on such short acquaintance. He couldn't have rated her highly to think she would jump into bed with him the third time they met. Not that it seemed like only their third encounter. For a second or two, in his arms, she had felt strangely at home. But perhaps that was just because she had spent so many wakeful nights with an imaginary lover with strong arms and warm lips but a face she could never see clearly.

The wake-up call organised, she got ready for bed, lay down and turned out the light. 'If you can sleep,' he had said, knowing that, even if she denied it, she had wanted him and still did.

The frissons she had experienced earlier this evening were as nothing to what she felt now. Every nerve in her body seemed to be clamouring for his touch. Against her will, she tried to imagine him making love to her. But she couldn't. She had no idea what he would be like as a lover, except that he would be different from the men she had known and now wished she hadn't.

No, that wasn't quite true. She could never regret the circumstances that had given her Dan.

Alex had had a cold shower and now was reading in bed but finding concentration difficult. He didn't regret making his move too soon because at least it had proved that she wanted to go to bed with him even if her moral code forbade it.

He had felt the excited beating of her heart while he was holding her. Her arousal, if less obvious than his own, had been evident in her flushed cheeks and dazed expression. Had she really disliked what had happened, she would have looked very different and told him off far more sharply. The memory of that endearingly absurd protest, 'Dr Strathallen...please...' made him smile.

In a way he was glad she had turned him down...this time. If she had been a pushover, he knew he would soon have lost interest. He liked women with minds of their own who didn't just go with the flow.

Next morning Nicole had packed her things and was ready to go when she heard voices in the sitting room. One of the speakers was Alex but the language he was using wasn't English.

When, quietly, she opened the door she found him chatting to a couple of waiters. The conversation was obviously amusing them. All three were smiling, showing off their white teeth. Nicole had always thought good teeth an important asset. Dissatisfied with the treatment offered by her parents' elderly dentist, she was having her son's teeth looked after by a more up to date orthodontist. She wanted Dan to grow up with straight sexy teeth like Alex's.

He noticed her standing in the doorway. 'Good morning. Come and have breakfast.'

Reverting to the language he and the men had been using, he appeared to be thanking and dismissing them.

'Was that Hindi or Urdu?' she asked, as they left the room.

Alex drew out a chair for her. 'It was Hindi. Although they're written differently, there's very little difference between them in speech. You could compare them with American-English and the English spoken in England.'

Nicole had expected their conversation this morning to be constrained by what had happened last night. But as Alex was behaving as if nothing *had* happened, she made an effort to seem equally at ease.

'Tea or coffee?' he asked. 'I ordered both, not knowing which you preferred at this time of day.'

'Tea for me. What about you?'

'Coffee...when it's available.'' He glanced at the stainless steel watch on his left wrist. 'How long will it take you to pack?'

'I'm ready to go...apart from brushing my teeth again.'

He raised an eyebrow. 'What time did you get up?'

'An hour ago.'

Anticipating his next question and the provoking gleam in the eye that might accompany it, she focussed her attention on the tea he was pouring out for her rather than his face as he asked, 'Sleep well?'

'Yes, thanks. Did you?'

She expected a teasing answer such as 'Not as well as I might have done' and was grateful when he said only, 'I don't when the bed is too soft, but the beds here are firm. A lot of my nights are spent lying on a Therm-A-Rest.'

'What's that?'

'It's a thin mattress used by wilderness travellers. But when Prince Kesri hosts one of his Desert Stars expeditions, the guests sleep on camp beds in magnificent tents. They're paying big bucks and don't expect to have to rough it.'

'Tell me about Prince Kesri. Considering he'll be my employer, I know very little about him.'

Alex said, 'You'll be meeting him in a few hours and can form your own impression.'

It seemed an enigmatic answer. She wondered why he wouldn't share his own view of the Prince with her.

It wasn't until they reached the airport that she discovered they weren't catching a scheduled flight but were flying in the Prince's private aircraft piloted by Alex.

'No need to be nervous. I've been flying since I was eighteen,' he told her.

'I'm not nervous,' she assured him, wishing Dan were here to share the experience. 'How far is it from Delhi to Karangarh?'

'The rail journey, via Jodhpur, takes a day and a night. Only the toughest backpackers attempt the journey by bus. By air it takes about three hours. The aerial view of the fortress is something you won't forget.'

'How do you do, Miss Dawson? I'm delighted to meet you. Welcome to Karangarh.'

As he shook hands with her, Nicole thought she had never seen a more spectacularly handsome man than Prince Kesri. Only slightly shorter than Alex and equally broad of shoulder, he had the kind of looks that would easily have brought him stardom in films or TV, or male supermodel status in the magazine world, if his role in life hadn't been fixed before he was born.

He had charm as well, oodles of it. But, for her, he lacked something that Alex had, something hard to define but even more noticeable when they were standing near each other. She had no doubt that most other women would unhesitatingly vote for the Prince if asked to make a choice between them. Even without his title and his extraordinary inheritance, he would have been highly eligible. But strangely, despite his status, he didn't have Alex's inherent air of authority, the steel she felt was the core of his personality.

Over a delicious lunch in the comfortable informality

of his private quarters, the Prince proved himself an amusing and relaxed companion. It was soon apparent that he and the Scot were on very close terms with each other.

After one cup of coffee, Alex excused himself, saying he had things to do. Taking this as a signal for them both to leave, Nicole rose.

'No, no, don't go yet, Nicole.' At the beginning of the meal the Prince had asked her permission to use her first name. 'I'd like you to stay a little longer.'

His first question, when they were alone, was, 'Am I right in thinking you're a little nervous of Alex?' Before she could answer, he went on, 'I've heard him described as formidable and sometimes he can be...particularly with pretty women. There is a reason for that which, when you've been here longer, I will tell you. In the meantime, don't be upset if at times he seems brusque and offhand. His bark is much worse than his bite...unless someone really gets on the wrong side of him and I'm sure you will never do that.'

'I hope not,' she said, intensely curious to know more about the reason he had mentioned.

She wondered how the Prince would react if he knew that, far from being offhand, his friend had already made a pass at her.

'We met at Eton,' he went on. 'I was miserably homesick. I hated the weather and the food. I longed for the sun and the colourful world I was used to. Alex was the only person who understood how I felt. He helped me through that bad time. I am forever in his debt. Now let me show you the rooms we have prepared for you. I hope *you* won't be homesick.'

'I'm sure I shan't, Your Highness.'

'There's no need to be formal when we're in private.

My staff and the people of Karangarh continue to address me as they did my father and grandfather. Officially, the princely order was abolished in 1971. But old customs die hard...especially in places as remote as this.'

Later that afternoon Nicole was lying on the sofa in her sitting room when there was a knock at the door.

Not knowing the Hindi equivalent of 'Come in', she swung her feet to the floor, intending to admit whoever was there. She was halfway across the room when Alex came in.

'Hello...how are you getting on?'

'Finding it hard to adjust to acres of space. This room...a bedroom and bathroom...a studio twice this size...plus my own private roof garden *and* a balcony. My background is middle-class suburbia. This is all rather overpowering.'

As she spoke she remembered that, like the Prince, Alex had been educated at England's most exclusive public school. Only the super-rich could afford to send their sons there. Although he himself seemed classless, lacking all trace of upper-crust snobbishness, his background might be rather grand.

'You'll soon get used to it. Have you met your maid yet?'

'No, but it must have been she who unpacked all my things while we were having lunch.'

On their arrival at the palace, at Alex's suggestion, she had given her keys to a dignified butlerish person.

'Her name is Tara which in Hindi means star. If you put out the clothes you want to wear this evening, by the time we get back she'll have pressed them.'

'Where are we going?'

'I'm taking you for a stroll through the old town, if that's OK with you. If it isn't just say no…as you did last night,' he added, his smile disarming her.

She decided to take it lightly. 'To a stroll I'll always say yes. I need to change my shoes. What sort of clothes ought I to wear this evening?'

'We'll be eating à deux at the hotel. The dress code is what's called "smart casual". The skirt and shirt you wore last night would be fine.'

'Won't you sit down? I shan't be long.'

Nicole went through to the bedroom. When she looked in the large free-standing wardrobe where all her clothes had been hung, she found some were missing, including the ones worn last night. Selecting another shirt and skirt, she spread them on the bed, then changed her soft-soled house shoes for a sturdier pair.

'Finding your way in and out of the palace can be a puzzle at first,' said Alex, when she rejoined him. 'Do you have a good sense of direction?'

'I think so, but it's never been seriously tested.'

'You'll soon learn the short cuts. This is a quick way to the ramparts of the city.'

By a network of passages and stairways he led her to a doorway to a courtyard and thence through another courtyard where, outside a door in the wall, they startled a man in a scarlet turban who had been dozing.

'The guardian of the door,' said Alex when, after he and the elderly Indian had exchanged friendly greetings, they left him to resume his nap when they were out of sight. 'It's hardly ever used. Basically he's one of the palace pensioners.'

'Prince Kesri told me you and he were at school together…that he used to visit your home and sometimes you came here.'

'Yes, we go back a long way.' He glanced down at her. 'Quite a heart-throb, isn't he?'

'Very good-looking and charming,' she agreed. 'Why isn't he married?'

'Because for the time being he prefers to play the field,' Alex said dryly. 'There's a new intake of guests arriving this evening. You'll see him in action...if the women include someone he fancies. In public life he's an ardent reformer, in private an ardent womaniser. Don't say you haven't been warned.'

'It sounds as if you're two of a kind.'

'We're close friends...we're not alike. If anything we're opposites.'

She couldn't resist retorting, 'You certainly gave the impression of being a womaniser last night.'

'Are you trying to convince me you'd rather I didn't find you attractive?' he asked. 'I don't buy that, Nicole. You feel the same way that I do. The attraction is mutual, as these things usually are. A one-sided attraction is rare. Tell me, hand on heart, that you don't feel a thing and I'll back off and stay backed off.'

She couldn't and he knew she couldn't.

She said, 'I'm here to work, not to have an affair. I have room in my life for friendships, but not for a casual liaison which is what you have in mind. That sort of thing doesn't interest me. I would rather wait until I meet someone I can care for in the fullest sense. Physical attraction doesn't last long.'

'Are you speaking from experience?'

'Since you ask—yes. But I don't want to discuss it.'

'All right, we'll drop the subject. If friendship is what you want, friendship is what you shall have.' He broke his leisurely stride to offer her his hand. 'Let's shake on it.'

Deep in her heart, Nicole felt a pang of dismay. Though she didn't like to admit it, even to herself, this was more than she had bargained for. But having more or less demanded them, she couldn't reject his terms.

'Good…that's fine…thank you,' she said awkwardly, placing her hand in his.

As his long fingers closed over hers, she remembered feeling them at the nape of her neck last night. Her heartbeat quickened. Forcing herself not to pull her hand free and reveal to him how much even this casual contact affected her, she waited until he released it and they moved on.

The ramparts surrounding the fortress gave a bird's-eye view of the less picturesque town that had grown on one side of the old city. But from other parts of the ramparts the new town was lost to view. There was only the desert stretching into the far distance, unchanged since the fortress was built eight hundred years before.

'It's been called the city at the end of the world,' said Alex. 'The rulers of this and the other medieval forts were known as the wolf packs of the desert.'

As he talked about Karangarh's violent but colourful past, she had the feeling that he would have preferred those adventurous times to the era he lived in. Most of the men she encountered were domesticated animals who spent their days behind desks and their evenings watching television. Alex was different. It wasn't hard to visualise him with a sword in his hand, or directing the ambush and capture of one of the great caravans traversing the ancient trade routes.

*   *   *

That evening, in the part of the palace now converted into a hotel, they attended a drinks party for a group of twenty-four Americans. The room where this took place had been furnished in the 1930s in the then fashionable art deco style. There were many silver-framed photographs of Prince Kesri's grandfather and his family and signed photographs of foreign royalties and famous people of the period.

These caused excited murmurs among the Americans who were obviously thrilled to be socialising with a prince, even if his hereditary title was no longer recognised officially. Kesri, she noticed, made a point of having a few words with everyone, including her.

'Is your Internet connection working, Nicole?'

He himself, after showing her her quarters, had sat down with her notebook computer and keyed in the different settings that would allow her to use the Indian service provider that he, his staff and Alex used.

'Yes, thank you. I picked up some email from friends half an hour ago. Thank you for your help with that.'

'My pleasure,' he told her warmly. 'Had you come here fifty years ago, you would have waited months for a reply to a letter. A few years before I was born there was no proper road to Karangarh. I was five when the railway came. As long as we can hold out against a public airport, we shall remain comparatively unspoiled.' Smiling, he moved away to talk to an elderly man.

On the other side of the room Alex was listening to an American matron extolling the wonders of Jodhpur, the place they had come from.

Outwardly attentive to her chatter, he was actually thinking about Nicole, wondering why he had committed himself to treating her as a friend. Earlier in the day it had been his intention, after dinner, to escort her back to her rooms via various romantic parts of the palace where he had intended to melt away her defences.

Now he had given his word that he wouldn't do that. He must have been out of his mind.

That two of the Americans were accompanied by an attractive daughter who had already given him the eye did nothing to lessen his annoyance with himself. It was Nicole he wanted and was determined to have, knowing that once she let down her guard, they could have a wonderful time together.

Perhaps, if he could win her confidence by treating her like one of his sisters for a while, he could get her to confide the reason she couldn't relax and enjoy her sexuality.

CHAPTER FOUR

WHEN everyone moved into the courtyard for dinner, the Americans were seated in groups of eight, four on each side of the table with an empty chair at the head of it. Alex and Nicole had a table to themselves.

'Kesri will sit with each group for one course,' Alex explained to her.

What he did not add was that the women who would be sitting next to the Maharaja were the pick of the bunch in terms of looks, Nicole noticed. While passing one of the tables she had noticed place cards, so this arrangement hadn't happened by chance. Whoever had set out the cards must have guessed, or been told, who the Maharaja would wish to have beside him.

Alex was as good as his word. Not once during dinner did his conversation or manner go beyond the bounds of friendliness.

After dinner some dancers gave a short performance. When it ended, he said, 'I expect you'd like an early night. Can you find your way back to your room? If you're not sure, I'll ask someone to take you.'

'Thank you, but I don't think I'll get lost. Goodnight, Alex.'

'Goodnight.'

She had the feeling that as soon as she had departed he would join the others and not give her another thought. Whereas she was torn between relief that he had stopped pursuing her and regret that she had put him off.

* * *

During her first week at the palace, both Kesri and Alex spent time showing Nicole round.

Alex took her into town, introduced her to some of the shopkeepers and acted as her interpreter. He also explained Karangarh's major problem.

'Like all the desert forts, it's built of sandstone on a base of sand, clay and rock. In the old days, the only drainage was by open gulleys down the sides of the streets. There was very little waste water. Now the population is growing and using more water. It's having the same effect as when a child tips a bucket of water over a sandcastle.' He made a graphic gesture with the shapely hands that were one of his many attractions for her.

'Can't the drainage be improved?' she asked.

'Sure, but it takes time and money. Meanwhile there's water seeping away where it shouldn't, saturating the whole basic structure. In places the city wall has burst open. Some of the bastions are unstable. More than a hundred buildings are in various stages of collapse. For some of them it's too late.'

'That's terrible!' she exclaimed.

'It would have helped if the restoration programme had been started by Kesri's grandfather,' Alex said dryly. 'Some of the old maharajas were enlightened rulers, and some of them weren't.'

Another day he took her to see some of the mansions called *havelis*, some ruined beyond repair and some under restoration. The houses were built from thick blocks of honey-coloured sandstone with the decorative parts carved from limestone.

'They didn't use mortar,' said Alex. 'The panels were held in place by stone keys or cramps made of iron. So parts of the ruined houses can sometimes be salvaged and used in the restorations.'

Standing behind her, he put one hand on her left shoulder and stretched his other arm over her right shoulder the better to point out where this work had been done.

Had it been anyone else, she would hardly have noticed, her attention being focussed on the building. But because it was Alex, she did. The light touch of his fingers and thumb felt as if they were five separate contacts through which, at any moment, she would feel an electric charge. She was also intensely conscious of his tall powerful frame stationed close behind her slighter softer body; so close that if she leaned back, even an inch or two, her shoulder-blades would touch his chest.

The disturbing thing was how much she wanted to lean back, to be enfolded by strong arms. Doubly disturbing was that he might sense her reaction.

It was a relief when they moved on to look at another building.

Although busy, the Maharaja made time to show her some of his family treasures. They included a solid silver dining table with a shimmering pattern of waves on its surface and a drinking cup carved from a single emerald. He also discussed the work he had hired her to do.

'We have first-class craftsmen of many kinds, but we lack designers who can invent new ways to use the traditional skills,' he told her.

As her body adjusted to being in a different time zone, Nicole was able to stay up later at night, sometimes writing long emails to Dan and her girlfriends, sometimes working on ideas in her new studio.

At the end of that week Alex announced he was leaving. Until he mentioned that he would be back in a few days, she thought he might be gone for weeks, even months, and was surprised how much she minded the prospect of not having him around.

He did not tell her where he was going, or why, and instinct restrained her from asking. It wasn't her business and she sensed that he was a man who would resent being questioned. If he wanted her to know he would tell her. Otherwise it was politic to hold her tongue.

One day during his absence she couldn't help reminding the Maharaja of what he had said about a reason why Alex was sometimes 'formidable' with young and attractive women.

'I wondered how long it would be before curiosity overcame you,' he said, with a mischievous look. Then his expression changed to gravity. 'At what is usually the most carefree time of a man's life, Alex went through an experience so terrible that it changed his whole personality. Up to that time he was the happiest person I've ever known. How much has he told you about his family background?'

'Nothing,' said Nicole. 'He's never mentioned it and I haven't asked.'

'His father is a Scottish landowner. He's an only son. One day, when his father dies, he'll have to return to Scotland and run the estate. Until that happens he's a free agent. Travelling and working in other parts of the world is a tradition in his family. His grandfather married a Hungarian countess he met while working in America. His great-grandfather also travelled and married a foreigner. But Alex's mother is Scottish…as was his wife.'

Nicole hoped he couldn't tell how shocked and dismayed she felt. 'His wife?' she echoed questioningly.

'They were both very young. He was twenty-one. Nuala was only nineteen. They'd known each other from childhood. Their families tried to persuade them to wait, but Alex was adamant. They were going to travel together and he felt, as his wife, she would receive more respect in countries with stricter codes than those in the west. He was right about that. In many countries, girls who travel alone, or with men they are not related to, are regarded by the local people as little better than—' His gesture left her to fill in the word he had omitted.

'What happened to her?' Nicole didn't want to know but was impelled to ask.

'They were in another part of India. As most backpackers do, sooner or later, Alex went down with a bug and had to stay in their room in a low-budget hotel. One morning Nuala went out to buy some things they needed. She was caught in one of the street riots that can erupt without warning when there's political unrest. She was hit by a hurled brick. It killed her. Alex couldn't forgive himself for taking her to that place.'

'How terrible.' She felt her eyes filling with tears at the thought of what he must have suffered. It would be like losing Dan, an unimaginable anguish, a wound that would never heal.

'You're very tender-hearted,' Kesri said, seeing her reaction.

Trying to control her emotions, she said huskily, 'Anyone's heart would bleed for them.'

'It was a tragic ending to their short time together.

But who knows, if she had lived, if they would still be together? Like others, I didn't think Nuala was right for Alex. She was stronger on charm than intelligence. He has a first-class brain. He picks up languages as easily as other people memorise tunes. Even at Eton he was said to have a better understanding of the nuances of Slavic grammar than his tutor.'

'I don't think people necessarily need matching brain power to be happy together,' said Nicole.

'Perhaps not in every case. But I've often seen Alex bored by women who chatter about trivialities in the same way Nuala did. She might have matured. She might not. The real tragedy is not that she died young but that it has spoiled his life. He can't forgive himself. As a self-punishment, he has renounced marriage and fatherhood. Even his duty to his line doesn't alter his determination never to marry again.'

'But that's crazy,' said Nicole. 'What good will it do?'

'None at all, but that's the way he sees things and no one will change his mind. Many women have tried. He'll indulge their desires, up to a point...but not to the extent of giving his heart to them. That part of his heart is dead. Now all he feels is affection for his friends and compassion for those in need.'

Perhaps he's like me, she thought. Perhaps he has never met another person he could love. She didn't share these thoughts with Kesri.

'It's a long time ago. I don't think it weighs on his mind as much as it used to,' the Maharaja went on. 'But it's always there in his subconscious. I wouldn't have told you about it except that when he is here you'll be seeing a good deal of each other. I should be sorry to see you hurt, Nicole. And that, I'm afraid, would be the inevitable outcome if you allowed yourself to become too fond of him.'

'There's no risk of that,' she said firmly.

For a moment she was tempted to tell him about Dan, but decided to put it off until she had been here longer.

Alex had been paying his last visit to an old man who had helped him to make important contacts at the start of his researches. Now Ajit was close to the end of his life and although he was cheerful about it, confident he would soon be starting another phase of his soul's long journey, Alex knew Ajit's death would leave an irreparable gap in his own life.

Driving his Jeep back to Karangarh, he found himself thinking about Nicole and wondering if she would stay or if, after the novelty had worn off, she would begin to miss what she had called 'middle-class suburbia'.

He remembered the expression on her face when she had emerged from the airport building at Delhi: the look of alarm and uncertainty until she had seen him. She had revived protective instincts he had re-trained to suit the era he lived in.

His parents tended to live in a time warp, especially his mother. When he was small, she had taught him that his sisters, and all girls, must be treated with care and, if need be, defended. But much had changed since her youth. Women today didn't need or want the kind of protection their mothers and grandmothers had expected. Nicole would have survived the hassle at the airport if he hadn't been there to extricate her. There was no need to treat her like one of the delicate sandstone cups carved by Jalgarpur's stone-carvers.

Tired by the long bumpy drive, and covered with dust from the desert tracks, as soon as he got back he went to his quarters for a refreshing shower. He would find out how Nicole had been getting on during his absence when they met at dinner.

Nicole had just opened her laptop to write an email to send later to Dan when there was a distinctive triple knock on the door. Only one person knocked like that. Quickly closing the notebook, she flew across the room to admit him.

'Oh…you're back,' she said, affecting surprise, concealing the pleasure she felt at the sight of his tall figure framed by the doorway.

'Hello, Nicole. May I come in?'

He greeted her pleasantly but not as if coming to see her had been a priority. For all she knew he might have come back at lunchtime. She had been busy working and had lunched in her studio on fruit and some curd from the ice box.

'Please do. How are you?'

'I'm fine. How have you been getting on?'

'I'm in designers' heaven. The colours…the patterns…the shapes. Come and look at some photos I've just had developed.'

She led him through to the studio where, on a side table, she had spread photographs of the many different patterns of the latticework screens that, originally, had allowed the women of the palace to look out without being seen by outsiders.

'And those aren't all the patterns, just the ones I could get on a thirty-six exposure roll of film.'

Alex cast an eye over the prints. 'Perhaps some time when we've both got a few days to spare you might like to fly over to Jodhpur and see the palaces inside Mehrangarh Fort. The latticework there is legendary. There are over two hundred patterns. An architectural historian said the whole building looked as if it were hung with lace.'

'I'd love to go...but, if you've seen it before, wouldn't going again bore you?'

'No one could be bored at Mehrangarh. It's a fantastic place.'

'This seems fantastic to me. Every day since you left either Kesri or his curator has taken me to see something amazing. Yesterday I was shown the collection of the rarest and most precious miniature paintings.'

'The palace is stuffed with treasures. Fortunately the dryness of the desert climate is less damaging than the dampness in some parts of India. Even so, things need looking after and Kesri has made sure they are. In his early twenties he was a bit of a playboy, but since he was twenty-five he's concentrated most of his energies on preserving and improving his heritage.'

Remembering what had happened to Alex in his early twenties, she felt a stab of pity. In a different way, her own dreams and hopes had been shattered. But she had had Dan to pull her through. Alex had had nothing to help him recover.

Her studio windows had glass and canvas awnings in place of latticework. Now the angle of the light reminded her that it would soon be the hour of the day when the golden stone of the fortress and the buildings it encompassed were given an apricot glow by the fiery desert sunset.

'Would you like a drink?' she suggested.

'Do you have any lager? If not, any long drink will

do. Driving around this terrain works up a powerful thirst.'

'I have some lager. I don't often drink it myself, but it seemed a good idea to have some for visitors.' She went to the fridge and took out a bottle for him and a can of tonic for herself.

'Let me do that for you,' he said, before she could decap the bottle. 'Are you having some gin with your tonic?'

'Yes, please.' There was gin and an unopened litre of whisky with the glasses on the drinks tray.

He dealt with the drinks and carried them through to the sitting room.

'Is that your father?' he asked, noticing the photograph she had placed on one of the tables.

'Yes, that's Dad in the garden before he developed health problems and had to take early retirement.'

There should have been a picture of Dan beside her father's photograph but, for the time being, she kept it in a locked drawer in the bedroom. She didn't want anyone to see it until she had explained her situation to Kesri. Somehow she had the feeling he would be understanding. How Alex would react she couldn't tell. She hoped it wouldn't make him think less of her. There were still some people, though not usually those under forty, who took a censorious view of single mothers who hadn't been widowed or divorced.

She had also found that some men assumed that if you had had a child outside wedlock you must have a particularly free and easy attitude to sex. Which, at least in her case, was the reverse of the truth. Being left to cope single-handed with the consequences of her first experience of making love hadn't made her eager for more. It left her deeply reluctant to attempt it again.

For four years after Dan's birth, she had been as chaste as a nun, only embarking on another relationship because her child needed a father.

'I needn't ask if this is your mother?' said Alex, picking up the second photograph. 'You're very alike.' He gave her an appraising look. 'Except that she doesn't have your obstinate chin.'

'I think it's a myth that features reflect people's characters. I used to work with a man who had a receding chin. He was as stubborn as they come. I know my chin is too square, but I'm not an obstinate person.'

'Aren't you?' He looked amused. 'You give a good imitation of being a woman who can't easily be persuaded.'

As she realised to what he was referring, she felt her colour rising.

Before she could answer, he went on, 'But your chin isn't *too* square. It redeems your face from being merely pretty and gives it character.'

'If that's a compliment…thank you.'

'The terms of our treaty don't preclude an occasional compliment, do they? I'm sure Kesri has made some comment on your beautiful skin, if only to warn you to protect it from the desert sun.'

'He did say I should be careful, but he was being thoughtful rather than complimentary. *He* has never stepped out of line by a centimetre,' she said pointedly. 'He may flirt with the guests at the hotel. That's different. I'm sure he wouldn't create an awkward situation for one of his employees.'

At that moment there was another knock at the door and Kesri himself walked in.

'I was told I would find you here,' he said to Alex. Then to Nicole, 'May I join you?'

'Of course. Would you like a drink?'

When she had fetched a gin and tonic for him, Kesri said, 'My sister Chandra is coming home for a few days. On the day she wants to come, the head of an important American travel company is arriving. I must be here to receive him. Could I ask you to fetch her, Alex? I can send Mohan if it's not convenient for you. But I know she would prefer your company.'

'I'd be delighted to fetch her,' said Alex.

'Thanks very much.' Kesri turned to Nicole. 'Mohan is a qualified pilot who also supervises the maintenance of the plane. He's a thoroughly reliable fellow but not much of a conversationalist. Chandra works hard and takes very little time off, so I like to make her visits here as pleasurable as possible. She'll enjoy the flight far more with Alex as her pilot.'

Alex said, 'Is there anything you'd like me to bring back from Delhi, Nicole? Anything to do with your work that you forgot to bring and won't be able to buy here?'

'I don't think so, but thank you for offering. What is your sister's work, Kesri?'

'She's a gynaecologist…and also deeply involved in various women's rights organisations. Raising the level of female literacy is one of her special concerns. And mine,' he added.

On the day of Kesri's sister's arrival, Nicole's maid brought her a note inviting her to join them for dinner.

Nicole decided to wear a dress she had designed and had made up by a friend she had met at pre-natal classes. Emily was also a single mother who, to support herself and her daughter, had built up a successful clothes alterations business. Now assisted by several part-timers and under less pressure, she also did high-quality dressmaking for Nicole and a few other customers with exciting ideas.

Nicole's dress was made from a length of exquisite printed silk-chiffon she had seen in an antiques shop and been unable to resist. The shop specialised in things made in the Thirties and Nicole's design for the chiffon was an echo of that stylish era.

When she was ready, she made her way to the room where the Maharaja had welcomed her on her first day at the palace. Already she felt at home. The only flaw in her contentment was missing Dan.

A turbanned servant was on duty outside the double doors of Kesri's drawing room. He opened them with a flourish, standing aside for her to enter.

There were only three people present: the two men she had expected to see and a woman who did not match her preconception of Kesri's sister. Somehow she hadn't expected Chandra to share her brother's good looks. He had made her sound a serious-minded and perhaps rather intimidating person. Which had not prepared Nicole for the glamorous vision in a pale blue sari and pearls who was smiling at her.

'Come and sit next to me,' said Chandra, when they had been introduced and Nicole had been given a glass of champagne.

Far from being formidable, her manner couldn't have been more friendly. Seeing her now, every inch an Indian princess in graceful traditional dress with real pearls at her ears and throat and a sapphire bracelet clasping one slender wrist, it was hard to imagine her in a white coat with a stethoscope in her pocket. The only clue to her occupation was that her nails did not extend beyond the tips of her fingers.

'While he was flying me home, Alex refused to tell me anything about you,' she said, as Nicole joined her on the sofa while the men sat in large armchairs placed at right angles to each end of it. 'He will never discuss other people, not even in a flattering way. I don't like unkind gossip, but he goes to the other extreme.' She flashed a teasing glance at him from her large and long-lashed dark eyes.

Then, concentrating her attention on Nicole, she said, 'What a lovely dress. Do you design your own clothes?'

One evening, when Nicole had opened her laptop with the intention of writing an email to Dan, the computer didn't go through its usual start-up process. The screen remained blank and, from somewhere inside the case, came a faint but ominous grinding sound.

She was too experienced a user to fly into panic immediately. After doing everything she could think of that might get it going, she consulted the manual and went through all the routines that were recommended. None of them did the trick.

Hoping whoever serviced the palace computers would be able to repair it for her, or at least point her in the direction of someone who could, she made herself a cup of tea and considered the situation. At worst, she might have to replace it, an expense and inconvenience she could do without. At best, whatever was wrong could be put right, but perhaps not for several days. In the meantime she might be able to borrow or rent a substitute.

But that didn't solve her immediate problem: how to send her nightly bulletin to Dan. As a last resort she could phone him, but calls from India to Europe were expensive and, before she could speak to him, she would have to waste several minutes listening to Rosemary who seemed unable to grasp that overseas calls were costly.

After more thought she decided to seek help from Alex. When she called his extension on the internal telephone, he answered with a brisk, 'Strathallen speaking.'

'It's Nicole. I hope I'm not disturbing you?'

'Not at all. What can I do for you?'

'My laptop seems to have died on me. I was wondering if you'd allow me to use your machine to pick up some important email.'

'By all means. Do you want to do it now?'

'If it's not inconvenient?'

'No, it's good timing. I've finished what I was doing. Bring the laptop with you. I might be able to resuscitate it. Do you know where to find me?'

'Yes...I'll be there in five minutes.'

She spent three minutes brushing her hair and re-touching her lipstick before hurrying from her part of the palace to the wing where she knew his rooms were. Now she would see for herself what personal imprint, if any, Alex had stamped on his living quarters. He had had them for a long time, but perhaps, like the nomads, he had few possessions. The bits and pieces she treasured, he might regard as clutter.

The door was already half open when she arrived. She tapped on the wood before she entered, closing the door behind her. He had called 'Come in' when she knocked, but when she passed through the hallway into his sitting room it was empty.

'I'll be with you in a minute,' he called, from another room.

Nicole stood looking around her. Every wall had been fitted with shelves to accommodate an extensive private library. In places half-height shelving left wall space for paintings hung frame to frame in a carefully thought out mosaic which took account of the colours as well as the shapes. He had not 'killed' the delicate watercolours by hanging them next to bigger and bolder acrylics.

She was pleased by his eclectic taste. It mirrored her own, except that his pictures had come from many parts of the world while the source of hers were junk shops and car boot sales.

She was scanning the spines of some of his books when Alex joined her.

'Do you have all these catalogued?' she asked.

He came to where she was standing, the laptop held on her hip. Taking it from her, he said, 'There is a catalogue, but I don't often have to use it. I can usually lay my hand on the book I want. They're arranged in categories...languages...outdoor sports...history et cetera.'

'Kesri told me you were a brilliant linguist.'

'He exaggerates. An ear for language is like an ear for music, or your eye for good design. It's something people are born with and can develop, or neglect, as the spirit moves them. A lot of Scots are good at picking up languages. It's one of our positive characteristics...a counterbalance to our reputation for meanness,' he added, smiling.

'There are unflattering myths about all nationalities. I think of the Scots as brave in battle and mad keen on higher education. But you're the first Scot I've had much to do with.'

'My PC is in my office. What makes you think this

is dead?' he asked, as he led the way to a smaller room where an L-shaped counter provided two separate work areas.

Nicole explained while taking in the well-organised layout of his working equipment.

'Is it still under guarantee?' Alex asked.

'Unfortunately, no. In fact this model is no longer being made. I'm overdue for an upgrade, but I've been putting it off. You know how it is with computers. You've no sooner bought one than the thing is obsolete.'

'Or so the manufacturers would like to have us believe,' he said dryly. 'Do you mind if I take a look at its innards?'

If anyone else had asked that, she would have demurred. But with Alex she knew instinctively that he wouldn't, like some of his sex, claim an expertise he didn't have.

'Go ahead,' she said. 'I never mess with the insides, although my...I know people who do.' She had stopped herself just short of saying 'my son does' and hoped that the hasty switch from 'my' to 'I' hadn't caught his attention.

'You sit here,' he said, pulling out the desk chair facing the screen of his desktop PC. 'I take it you're collecting and sending with one of the free mail services? I'll just get you connected and leave you to it.'

One hand on the back of her chair and his other hand on the mouse, he clicked his way through the Internet connection procedure. It seemed to take longer than usual. Or was that only because he was standing so close behind her? Nicole wondered. Instead of watching the screen, she looked at the strong sunburned hand sliding the mouse over the surface of the mouse-mat.

Each time his finger pressed the button, a sinew moved under the skin on the back of his hand. She liked the length of his fingers, his short well-kept nails, the light dusting of hairs on his muscular wrist.

She found herself wishing he would take his hand from the mouse and slide it under her chin, turning her face up to his, bending his tall frame to kiss her. She wanted it to happen so badly that when he started speaking she didn't take in what he was saying.

Collecting her scattered wits, she realised he had opened a screen from which she could access her mail service.

'It's all yours,' he said, moving away.

'Thank you,' she murmured, half relieved, half frustrated.

Her fingers unusually clumsy, she mis-typed the familiar address and had to re-type it. Then, as she keyed in her password, the surge of desire she had felt a few moments ago dissipated. Her thoughts focussed on the email she expected to find in her inbox.

Alex moved to the other work space. Before starting a check on Nicole's laptop, he spent a few moments studying her profile, knowing that, intent on the screen, she would not be aware of his scrutiny.

'If you want to print anything out, be my guest,' he said.

'Oh…thank you.' She flashed an abstracted glance at him, then returned her attention to the monitor.

He wondered who her correspondents were. Other designers…girlfriends…her father? From where he was leaning against the desktop he couldn't read the writing on the screen. But he could see from her face that whatever it was gave her pleasure. Her lips curled back from her teeth in a glowing smile. She had never smiled at him like that.

His gaze drifted down from her face to the hollow at the base of her throat and the vee of bare skin revealed by her white cotton shirt. It was fastened by little pearl buttons. He found himself wanting to undo them, to distract her from what she was doing as she was distracting him.

She was getting under his skin to an annoying extent. He knew that the only cure was to take her to bed, enjoy her and get her out of his system. Except that she wasn't the kind of woman with whom that way out was possible. She didn't want an affair. She wanted a man who would give her his heart and his soul, and he didn't have them to give.

The noise of the ink-jet printer interrupted his thoughts. He watched Nicole starting to touch type, a skill he had taught himself but without achieving the speed of her flying fingers.

He forced himself to stop watching her and turn his mind to what might be wrong with her laptop.

Nicole took the single sheet of paper from the out tray of Alex's printer and folded it in half, blank side outermost. She didn't want him to spot that the message began *Dearest Mum* and ended with a row of crosses followed by a row of paired brackets symbolising hugs.

Not that Alex would necessarily know about things like smileys and emoticons with which her son's generation peppered their emails.

'I've finished now, thank you. I'll disconnect…OK?'

'OK.' Intent on what he was doing, he didn't look round.

Nicole closed down the connection and spent a few

moments looking at the icons on the screen. They could be as revealing of people's habits and tastes as the contents of their cupboards and bookshelves.

Unlike Dan whose Windows desktop was crowded with numerous icons, many of them representing blood-and-thunder games, Alex had very few. Most were short cuts to folders in regular use. *Shortcut to lecture notes* and *Shortcut to typescript* were two that she noticed. She wondered if he was writing a book about the nomads, but didn't like to ask in case he preferred not to talk about it.

At that point his screen saver activated: a sequence of beautiful photographs epitomising Karangarh. A camel pacing slowly across the desert...a girl with her face concealed by a rose-pink veil and silver anklets adorning her bare brown feet...the city seen from a distance in the light of sunset.

'I think this problem is beyond me,' Alex said, shaking his head. 'You need someone more expert. At a guess I'd say your hard disk needs replacing, but I could be wrong. Anyway, as long as it's out of commission, you're welcome to come and use mine to get and send mail. How many times a day do you check your inbox?'

'Only once. But I don't want to impose on—'

'You won't be imposing,' he said firmly. 'You'd do the same for me if my system had crashed. Leave the machine with me and tomorrow I'll have it looked at. Would you like a drink?' The question was accompanied by a gesture towards the sitting room. 'I have a bottle of a very fine single malt whisky I think you'd find a surprise if you've only drunk blended whiskies.'

'This will probably damn me in your eyes for ever,

but the only whisky I've drunk has been with hot water and lemon as a cure for colds,' she admitted.

Alex laughed. 'Then it's high time you were taught to drink it properly. Make yourself comfortable and we'll share one of life's greatest pleasures...a wee dram.'

But the look he gave her before turning away suggested that it was another of life's pleasures he was thinking about. Or was that impression only a figment of her over-heated imagination? Nicole wondered, as she decided against sitting on the sofa and chose one of the several comfortable chairs grouped to face it.

CHAPTER FIVE

IF HE noticed her avoidance of the sofa, or if he too was reminded of her first night in India, it was impossible to tell.

She wondered how alcoholic the 'wee dram' would be. She didn't think Alex would renege on their treaty without warning. On the other hand he might take her acceptance of his invitation to stay for a drink as a sign that she had changed her mind.

From a cupboard he brought a bottle of whisky, another of water and two glasses which she would have thought were copitas for drinking sherry, except that these had a thicker base.

'You don't have to be a designer to know there are three primary colours, and most people know there are four primary tastes...sweet, sour, salty and bitter,' he said. 'But do you know how many primary aromas there are?'

'I've no idea. Six? Ten?' she guessed.

Alex shook his head. 'You're miles out. There are twenty-three. Sight is our dominant sense, but the nose is our most sensitive organ. I'm going to pour a little whisky in your glass. Sniff it and then take a very small sip. Then I'll add water to it. The water brings out the "nose".'

Nicole did as he told her and was astonished at the difference.

Alex settled himself in the chair nearest to hers and held his glass to the light to admire its pale golden colour. Then he put the glass to his nose and breathed in its fragrance before drinking.

'Did you know that, in the old days, most of the palaces in this part of India made their own liqueurs from closely guarded recipes? According to Chandra, a lot of secret drinking went on in the women's quarters.'

'I'm not surprised,' said Nicole. 'Who wouldn't take to the bottle, being kept shut away like that? Can you imagine someone like Chandra herself confined to a *zenana*? It would have driven her mad.'

It was more than an hour later before she suddenly realised how the time had flown.

'Goodness, I had no idea how late it was,' she said, after glancing at her watch.

'It's not *that* late,' Alex said lazily. He looked very relaxed, his long legs stretched out in front of him, one arm hanging over the side of his chair.

Tonight he reminded her not of a cheetah but a leopard. She had seen pictures of them stretched on the thick branches of trees, one front leg dangling like his arm. In that posture they looked as harmless as pussy cats. Not the lethal predators they could be.

Alex also had predatory instincts, even if he had kept them under wraps since their walk on the ramparts.

Part of her longed to linger, to have another small measure of the wonderfully smooth whisky, to continue a conversation that had already ranged over a broad spread of topics. But part of her knew that to stay was to risk giving the impression that, now they had known each other longer, she might be more responsive.

And in fact she *was* more responsive. The better she knew him, the more she liked him, the more potent his attraction became. It had been strong from the outset. Now it was even more powerful.

'No, but I must go. I have things to do,' she said, rising.

With the fluid ease of movement that went with his physical fitness, Alex stood up. 'What sort of things?'

'Oh…women's things…nails and so on. You don't know how lucky you are only having to shower and shave. It's much harder work being a woman,' she said, in a light-hearted tone. 'Anyway thanks a lot for letting me use your PC, and for the whisky. Don't bother to come to the door. Goodnight, Alex.'

But he came to the door and opened it for her. 'Goodnight, Nicole. If we don't meet during the day, I'll see you tomorrow night.'

The problem with her computer remained unresolved for some days. One computer engineer agreed with Alex's diagnosis. Another said no, it was a fault with the motherboard. Both took the view that it was not worth replacing the damaged parts. Both said the purchase of a new machine was the only sensible solution.

'Before you do that, there's someone else I can try,' said Alex. 'He's the student son of a shopkeeper in the new town. The boy knows a lot about all electronic gadgets. I'll ask him to take a look.'

'I'm putting you to a great deal of trouble.'

'No problem.'

His tone dismissed her concern as unnecessary. Yet instinct told her that he wasn't pleased about something. Each night when she picked up her email, he offered her a glass of whisky and she accepted and they talked.

But each night she had the feeling that he wished he

hadn't started the ritual, an impression reinforced by the fact that when she got up to go he didn't attempt to detain her.

As he waited for Nicole to emerge from his office after picking up her email, Alex had little doubt she was corresponding with a man. She wouldn't look so pleased with herself if the emails were coming from girlfriends. They had to be coming from someone important to her. But for reasons best known to herself she was keeping quiet about it.

Perhaps the guy was someone who had picked her up in an Internet chat group and she didn't like to admit to it. Or perhaps he was someone she had known before coming to India who was missing her more than he had expected to.

Whoever he was, his emails gave her a noticeable glow. It was not beyond the bounds of possibility that she had taken this job mainly to bring him up to scratch. One of Alex's sisters had done that: taken a job in London and pretended to be having a ball there because Rob McLaren wasn't taking as much interest in her as she wanted him to. The strategy had worked. Within six months Rob had followed her to London and asked her to marry him. Which might never have happened if Alice hadn't cut loose and stopped him taking her for granted.

If Nicole was trying the same thing, it would make him revise his initial opinion of her as someone straightforward and trustworthy. She had given the impression that she really wanted this job and was prepared to invest a sizeable chunk of her future in it.

Tonight, as on previous nights, she emerged from the office with the air of a woman who has just received at least one message of more than ordinary importance.

'Is there any news about my laptop?' she asked.

'Not yet. Perhaps tomorrow.'

Alex watched her sit down, wondering how long it would be before she got up again, claiming urgent things to do but actually, he suspected, impatient to reread the email she had printed out.

As he poured out their drinks, she said, 'Today it suddenly came to me what this whisky reminds me of...the old-fashioned butterscotch that a neighbour of ours used to make at Christmas time. Is it sacrilege to compare fine whisky with toffee?'

'Not at all. Depending on the part of Scotland it comes from, whisky has been compared to all kinds of things...humbugs...peardrops...even ginger snaps.' Watching her closely, he changed the subject. 'Did you get a reply to that long message I heard you rattling out last night?'

She seemed surprised that he had noticed. Having nothing better to do, he had timed the sound of her fingers flying over his keyboard. She had typed without pause for three minutes and seventeen seconds, time enough to cover several pages for the recipient to print out. Usually emails were brief, more like notes than letters.

'Yes, I did, thank you,' she said. 'I—I was writing about Karangarh. There's so much to describe.'

There was a perceptible awkwardness in her manner, as if she guessed he was curious and was nervous of being asked questions she would prefer not to answer.

He decided to put her on the spot by asking pointblank if it was her father she had written to at such length. He was certain it had not been her father and wanted to see if she would be frank or evasive.

To Nicole's dismay, Alex asked, 'Were you writing to your father?'

It would have been easy to say yes but, except to spare someone's feelings, she didn't like telling lies. For some reason lying to Alex was especially unacceptable.

'I write to Dad on Sundays. He doesn't have a computer, but another relative does and they print out my emails for him.'

'So who is the lucky recipient of all the weekday emails?'

'I write to several people.'

'But mainly to one special person?'

'Yes,' she agreed uneasily, wondering why he was pressing her.

'So the impression you gave in your answers to the questionnaire, that you had no personal commitments, wasn't strictly true?'

Nicole began to lose her cool. 'Are you implying that I lied?'

'Did you?'

Like a brushful of pigment dropped into water, hot colour spread from her jawline to her cheekbones. 'I have no commitments that prevent me doing a good job here. That was all you needed to know.'

When he didn't answer, she added, 'There are areas of people's lives they're entitled to keep to themselves. I'm sure you must have some in yours.'

In her anger at his probing questions, for an instant she had forgotten the deeply distressing nature of his most closely guarded feelings. She would have given a great deal to retrieve the last part of her hasty riposte, but the words had been spoken and could not be recalled.

His face took on the expression she remembered from when she had asked if his wife liked living in India, and again when she'd mentioned the Taj Mahal to him. He and the girl he had married must have been there together.

His tone cold as steel, he said, 'Doesn't your boyfriend mind playing second fiddle to your career?'

'He isn't my boyfriend.'

If he hadn't been furious with her, she would have told him the truth. But clearly this wasn't the moment. Already alienated by her thoughtless remark, he would see her deception in the worst possible light.

'He...he is someone I care for, but not in the way you're implying.'

'I hope you've made that clear to him. The frequency of your emails might make him think otherwise.'

'It isn't that sort of relationship.'

'You mean he's not interested in women?'

The design world was full of men who weren't. It seemed an easy way out of a tricky situation.

'No, he isn't,' she agreed.

At that point his telephone rang.

It was Kesri, asking if Alex was busy or if he could come and discuss an idea he'd had.

'By all means,' said Alex, pleased to find that his suspicion had been wide of the mark.

He didn't tell Nicole that Kesri was about to join them. If he did, she would seize on it as a reason to gulp down her drink and take off. If Kesri's idea was something confidential, he wouldn't have to reveal it in front of her. If it was not, she might have some useful input to contribute.

In the time they had spent together since the crash of her laptop, she had put forward several unexpectedly original perspectives. On the whole he found that women—or at least the ones he encountered—didn't spend a lot of time thinking about the more serious issues confronting the human race. Unless they were academics with a professional interest, most women seemed to take the view that they couldn't influence events so there wasn't much point in working out their opinions.

Nicole wasn't like that. She had opinions on most things. They didn't always coincide with his own, but at least she knew why she held them and could back them up with sensible arguments. She was the most intelligent woman he had met in a long time. In fact she was the first woman whose mind he found as attractive as her body.

When Kesri joined them, Nicole would have left but he insisted she must stay.

'I came to confer with Alex about my latest brainwave. Now I can confer with you both which is even better.' He sat down on the sofa. 'It's good to relax. It has been one of those days when I haven't had a moment's peace. Yes, some whisky would be most welcome, Alex.'

Again Nicole thought how handsome he was with his black hair and burnished bronze skin. He was much better-looking than Alex, yet for her he was not as attractive.

'What's this brainwave?' Alex asked him.

'You know how successful the Desert Stars trips have proved. But they appeal mainly to older people who have the money and the time to spend on rather special holidays. I would like to attract younger people. They would also have to be well-heeled, but there are plenty of Thirtysomethings making a lot of money in the financial and electronic industries. What if we were to provide a Desert Honeymoon?'

'On a two-at-a-time basis, it would only be economic if you charged a colossal price,' said Alex. 'Also, if you're aiming it at the American and Euro markets, you'd better research the wedding statistics among your potential customers. The media give the impression that marriage as an institution is in its death throes. It would only be the so-called ''power couples'' who could afford that kind of extravagance. Do they get married these days? Or do they live together to spare themselves aggro when the inevitable split comes?'

'That's a terribly cynical outlook,' Nicole protested. 'I'm sure the statistics would show that most people still get married and a lot of them stay married. How would a Desert Honeymoon tour differ from the regular Stars tours, Kesri?'

'The idea has only just come to me. I haven't worked out the details. Perhaps we would give them a larger and more luxurious tent. Obviously their privacy would be more important than on the regular tours. It might even be possible to give them the illusion of being alone in the desert without loss of service and security. If you were getting married, would a honeymoon in the desert appeal to you, Nicole?'

She thought about it before answering. For her a honeymoon seemed as unlikely as a trip to the moon.

'I don't think I'd mind where we went. The only

important thing would be to be together. But there are a lot of people for whom big weddings and honeymoons in glamorous locations are important status symbols. I'm sure there's a market for your idea, Kesri.'

'I think so too. But Alex has raised some valid points. I'd like you both to give it more thought.' To his friend, he added, 'You made a lot of useful comments when we were planning the regular tours.'

Nicole drank the last of her whisky. 'If you'll excuse me, I'll say goodnight.'

Neither man tried to detain her. With their usual meticulous manners they both rose to their feet. Alex came to the door with her.

As she walked along the corridor, she wondered if, now she had gone, they were talking about her and what they were saying. She felt reasonably sure that Kesri thought well of her. But she had an uneasy feeling that her relationship with Alex, having passed through a more comfortable phase, was now reverting to quicksand. Earlier, before Kesri joined them, they had been on the verge of a row.

It was Dan himself who forced Nicole to stop putting off the moment when she asked Kesri for permission to have her son with her for the holidays. Shortly after her laptop had been returned to her in perfect working order, Dan sent her an email telling her about a website on the Internet where amazingly cheap air fares were on offer.

There are some cool deals, Mum, he wrote. *Have a look when you're next online.*

She did and knew he was right in urging her to snap up a bargain. She also knew it was foolish to go on delaying. But it wasn't telling Kesri that worried her. It was how Alex would react that had made her procrastinate.

After writing a note to Kesri, saying there was something important she wanted to discuss with him, she gave it to Tara to deliver to one of the Maharaja's attendants. Within the hour, one of them came to fetch her.

Kesri was in his office reading a document. He rose to greet her, leaving his desk and indicating two comfortable chairs with a low table in front of them.

'How can I help you, Nicole?'

She waited until they were both seated before, looking directly at him and coming straight to the point, she said, 'I have a son called Dan. He's at boarding-school in England. I'd like your permission to bring him here for the holidays.'

As he seemed too taken aback to reply, she went on, 'You may feel that I should have made this clear before. But I felt it might jeopardise my chance of being appointed and I wanted this job very much.'

Kesri recovered from his astonishment. He said, 'How old is he?'

'Just thirteen.'

'I don't remember your exact date of birth, but you must have been very young when he was born.'

'I was nineteen.'

'And his father?'

'He was the same age as I was. We—we were never married.'

She hoped he would accept the way things were and not want to know all the details.

'I see,' he said, after a pause.

But Nicole felt that he couldn't possibly see. What

had happened to her was so alien to his own culture, at least as far as women were concerned. She had heard that in Bombay, the hub of the Indian film industry, there was a section of society where young women were more sexually emancipated than in other cities. But everywhere else there were strict rules which girls were content to obey. They included no sex before marriage.

'Certainly you may have your son to stay with you,' said Kesri.

Although he was giving permission, it was hard to tell what he was thinking. Had she fallen in his estimation? Perhaps when he had been at university in England, later going on to Harvard, he had had casual love affairs with British and American girls. But probably, in his heart, he had compared them unfavourably with the chaste girls of his own culture.

To her relief, all he said was, 'Do you have a photo of your son?'

Luckily she had her small shoulder bag with her and was able to produce a snapshot of Dan taken during her last days at home.

Kesri studied it. 'He looks a fine boy. Is he clever...athletic...or both?'

'He's average at everything but one thing...computer technology. He wants to be a software designer.'

'You say he's at boarding-school. That must be a strain on your resources, or does his father help you with his education?'

'My father is paying for his education. We don't have any contact with Dan's father.'

Again Kesri said, 'I see,' but she felt sure he didn't. It wasn't an understandable situation: a father and son who had nothing to do with each other. Dan knew his father's name but not that now he was better known by another name.

Her father was adamantly opposed to his grandson being told that the man who had opted out of his parental responsibilities had become the idol of millions of teenagers and showed no sign of losing his appeal to the young even now that he was on the wrong side of thirty.

'Please don't think that, when he's here, I won't give my full attention to my work,' Nicole went on. 'Dan is a very independent boy. He'll be perfectly happy to amuse himself while I'm busy. I've never had to organise a programme of entertainments for him in the holidays, the way some parents do. He loves reading. When he's not got his nose in a book, he'll be perfectly happy exploring.'

'I'm sure you are far too conscientious, and too interested in your work, to neglect it,' he said. 'Does he ride? No? Then perhaps he would like to learn. It can be a useful accomplishment.'

At that point his secretary came in with a document the Maharaja had asked him to find. Nicole took the hint that it was a busy day and she had been fitted in but should not stay too long. She thanked Kesri and left, much relieved that her 'secret' was out and had been received more calmly than she had expected.

Now all she had to do was to tell Alex.

She was having her lunch break when he came storming into the studio.

'Why the hell didn't you tell me?' he demanded.

She had anticipated that he wouldn't be pleased, but she hadn't foreseen this eventuality.

'Hello, Alex. Do come in,' she said pleasantly. 'Tell you what?'

'You know what I'm talking about. I don't like being taken for a ride. This is something you should have made clear from the outset.'

She met his angry glare calmly, determined not to be upset. 'I really don't see why. It has nothing to do with my professional qualifications. Kesri isn't fussed about it. Why should you be?'

It was plain that he was enraged, his control of his temper close to snapping point. 'You lied by default,' he accused her. 'You knew I wouldn't have backed your application if you had told me the truth.'

Nicole's chin lifted. Her lips firmed. 'Why wouldn't you have backed it?' she challenged him.

It was obvious from his hesitation that he hadn't thought the thing through. Kesri had mentioned the matter to him and Alex had shot round to see her without working out why he was angry and giving himself time to calm down.

'A mother's place is with her child,' he said curtly. 'Has it occurred to you that, if your son had an accident, there's no way you could reach him quickly?'

It had not only occurred to her, it was a waking nightmare that she had difficulty pushing to the back of her mind.

'Of course I've thought about that,' she said impatiently. 'But people can't let their lives be governed by worst-case scenarios. I weighed all the pros and cons and concluded that taking this job would be best for me…and for my son. He's at an excellent boarding-school, his grandfather lives nearby and Dan and I write every day. If we hadn't been able to do that, I probably wouldn't have applied for a job overseas. But with email, distance doesn't matter. We're in touch with each other on a daily basis.'

Alex continued to glower. 'All that doesn't alter the fact that you were behaving dishonestly by keeping silent about him. I thought better of you.'

The sting of contempt in his tone hurt her more deeply than she was prepared to admit. It also lit the fuse of her temper. 'No, you didn't,' she told him hotly. 'You never thought well of me. If you had, you wouldn't have tried to get me into bed with you at the Imperial. If you'd known that I had a child, you'd have made yourself even more objectionable. You'd have told yourself I was begging for it. I've met men like you before.'

This was completely unjust and she knew it as she was saying it. He was nothing like the men who had made unwelcome passes at her. Nor had he done a thing that, at her most primitive level, she hadn't welcomed.

'And hate our guts...is that what you're trying to tell me?' he asked, coming closer. 'One of us let you down and you hate the entire male sex. Especially me because, though wild horses wouldn't make you admit it, you wanted to be in my bed as much as I wanted you there.'

To be taunted with the truth was more than she could bear. In a reflex she hadn't known was in her, she brought up her hand in the age-old response of a woman goaded beyond endurance.

In an even faster reflex, Alex caught hold of her wrist and stopped her palm reaching its target.

'Denials are a waste of breath. I know and you know it's true...and very easy to prove.'

He swept her into a crushing embrace and brought

his mouth down on hers. For a few seconds she resisted. Then, knowing it was futile, she surrendered.

Afterwards she had no idea how long they lasted, those fiercely passionate moments in his arms. She felt he despised her and desired her in equal measure, but she didn't care. Nothing mattered but the feel of his powerful body and the sensuous warmth of his lips to which her lips were responding as eagerly and freely as if they were husband and wife, reunited after a long separation.

That, all the time they were kissing, was exactly what it felt like; the coming together of two halves now made one. She couldn't believe that their anger could, by fusing, become something different, something exquisitely pleasurable. But she had to believe it because it was happening and if it went on much longer she was going to…

And then, at the precise moment when she recognised the quivering of her thighs and other unfamiliar sensations as signals of losing control even more catastrophically, Alex released his hold and put her away from him.

He was barely in control himself. That much was obvious from his breathing and the blaze she could see in his normally cool grey eyes.

'I'm sorry.' His voice was rough with violent emotion. 'I didn't intend to do that. But the treaty we had couldn't have lasted much longer. The sooner I get back to the desert, the better for both of us.'

He turned and walked out of the room.

Alex was still in the desert when Dan arrived.

The day before, Nicole was flown to Delhi by Kesri's pilot. She spent the night at his sister's apartment in New Delhi, the modern part of the capital. Next morning they both went to the airport to meet Dan.

It took all Nicole's self-control not to weep with joy at the sight of her son. He had shot up at least an inch since they said goodbye. When they had finished hugging, she introduced him to Chandra, glowing with maternal pride as he pressed his palms together and bowed his head respectfully before taking the hand she offered him.

'Should I have touched her feet?' he asked later, when Chandra had left them and they were waiting to board the Maharaja's plane.

'I don't think so. It's a lovely gesture of respect from young Indians to their elders, but as far as I know it's not customary for foreigners to do it...unless they're presented to someone *very* old and venerable,' said Nicole.

With Dan sitting next to the pilot, she occupied one of the seats in the aircraft's small main cabin. From the air, most of the terrain they flew over between Delhi and Karangarh looked like a barren and empty landscape traversed by a few roads. But in one of the conversations during their friendly phase Alex had told her that this was a false impression. Had they been driving across this apparently deserted countryside, and had they stopped in what seemed like the middle of nowhere, a surprising number of people would suddenly have materialised to stare with uninhibited curiosity at the strangers passing through their territory.

Like her, Dan hadn't slept during the flight from London. By the time they reached the palace he was covering huge yawns and looking cross-eyed with tiredness. When she suggested a nap, he agreed that he was sleepy.

It was early evening when Nicole went to his room to wake him for supper. Like all boys of his age, he was sleeping so deeply that only a shaking would rouse him. She sat on the side of the bed, gazing at his unconscious face. It had lost the rounded contours of childhood and was beginning to show the first hints of how he would look in maturity, although his full lips and long eyelashes would not change for a while yet.

She thought of Alex's mouth as it was now and wondered what he had looked like at thirteen. She would ask Kesri if he had any photos of himself at Dan's age. They might include shots of Alex. When would he come back? What would his attitude to Dan be?

Dismissing Alex from her thoughts, she put her hand on Dan's shoulder and gently shook him awake.

They talked without pause for the rest of the evening until it was time for them both to go to bed.

To Nicole's delight, everyone who came into contact with her son seemed to find him as lovable as she did. She had prepared him for the fact that he might find gestures of friendliness and affection more vigorous than similar gestures in the west.

It was as well that she had. In his first few days at the palace, he received several pokes in the ribs and good-natured slaps that were actually intended as pats. He took them all in his stride, his natural friendliness and interest in everything around him making the transition easier than if he had been a shyer, less confident boy.

Dan had been at Karangarh for a week when Alex returned. Chandra and one of her aunts were spending a few days at the palace. They both had brief speaking parts in a new promotional video Kesri was having made.

Nicole and Dan and the video team had been invited to dinner and were having drinks beforehand when Alex walked in. Nicole didn't know at first that he had arrived because she was chatting to Chandra. It was the way Chandra's face lit up that made Nicole glance over her shoulder and see him crossing the room to greet the elegant older woman who was wearing a lavender chiffon sari.

Nicole resumed her conversation with Chandra, as if his arrival was of no special importance to her. But in that momentary glimpse of the involuntary brightening of the other woman's eyes she had recognised love: a love that was normally masked but tonight, caught off guard, had revealed itself for an instant.

It was several minutes before Alex came over to join them. 'Good evening, ladies.'

His smile for Chandra was warm, but he didn't smile at Nicole. A rather formal inclination of the head was all she received from him.

'I've been talking to your son,' he told her.

'He's been looking forward to meeting you,' she answered calmly, though the memory of their last encounter made it difficult to maintain her composure. 'But I think his ideas about the desert are probably far more romantic than the reality.'

'At Dan's age Alex and Kesri were full of romantic ideas,' said Chandra. 'They spent most of their time acting out stories from the past. I wasn't allowed to take part. I think it was being excluded from their exciting games that made me determined to become a doctor and to help other women have more control of

their lives. But we still have such a long way to go,'
she added, with a sigh.

Nicole felt a touch on her hand and found Dan standing at her elbow. She made room for him to join them,
resting her arm lightly on his shoulders. She felt Alex's
eyes on them, but Chandra had continued and Nicole
listened, pretending to be unaware of the male presence
on her right.

Chandra was still deploring the inequalities suffered
by many of her countrywomen when Kesri led them
through to the adjoining dining room where he indicated where he wished his guests to sit.

Nicole had her son on one side of her and the direc-
tor of the video on the other. On the other side of the
table Alex was seated between Chandra and her aunt.
During the meal they received more or less equal
shares of his attention, Nicole noticed. But even if he
would have preferred to spend all the time talking to
Chandra, politeness would have obliged him to make
himself equally agreeable to the older woman. When
he was listening to Chandra, it was impossible to tell
how he felt about her.

Perhaps if he realised she loved him, he might see
her in a new light. They had so much in common;
memories going back to their schooldays, the same
deep commitment to India. It might be that Chandra
was the one woman who could thaw his frozen heart.

CHAPTER SIX

WHAT Nicole had not foreseen was that Dan would quickly decide Alex was hero material. She had thought her son would be more impressed by Kesri's past exploits as a polo player and skier. But it was Alex and his journeys in the desert whom he seemed to find more exciting than the Maharaja and his silver trophies.

Even more surprisingly, in view of her own strained relationship with him, Alex responded to Dan's interest, patiently answering his questions and spending time with him.

Late one afternoon, when she had spent the day working on designs for embroideries which combined traditional shapes with exportable colour combinations, Dan came rushing in to announce that, if she agreed, Alex was willing to take him into the desert.

'He thinks you may not say yes, but you will, Mum, won't you? I'll be OK with Alex. I want to go more than anything.'

'How long would you be gone?'

'Not long, only a few days. Think how educational it will be,' he said earnestly.

'All right, if you think you'll enjoy it.'

'Excellent!' He flung his arms round her. 'I knew you'd agree...can't think why he thought you wouldn't.'

Relieved that Dan's antennae had not picked up any signals that his new hero and his mother had fallen out with each other, Nicole said casually, 'Perhaps he thought I might not like your going off without me.'

'You could come with us…if you wanted to. I'll ask him, if you like?'

'No, no…I don't want to come. I have too much to do and it's a guys' thing anyway.'

Although Dan was used to her working during his holidays, she wished she could spend more time with him. Sometimes she found herself envying her grand-mother's generation who, if they had had careers, had usually put them on hold while their children were growing up. But even in those days a woman had needed a husband who was able to support her. Nicole's father had been willing to do that for her, but she hadn't felt comfortable with it. For the first four years of Dan's life, she had freelanced from home. Then he had started at play school and she had worked full-time, with her father minding his grandson when she wasn't there for him.

At the weekend they joined a picnic Kesri had ar-ranged for some visiting travel agents. Alex was also present.

The picnic took place at a small pleasure palace built by one of Kesri's ancestors on the shore of a small 'tank', the name for a man-made lake. They were hav-ing lunch in one of the airy sandstone pavilions over-looking the lake when the talk turned to the desert.

In a pause in the conversation, Dan turned to Alex and said, 'Could Mum come into the desert with us?'

She was about to say that she didn't have time when Kesri intervened. 'If you would like to go, Nicole, I'm sure Alex would be happy to take you.'

She saw a muscle flicker at the point of Alex's jaw and felt sure he was secretly annoyed at his friend's intervention. But he didn't allow his private feelings to show.

'As long as you're perfectly clear that it won't be a comfortable excursion...' he said, giving her a keen look. 'There are no mod cons where we're going.'

'I think I can cope with that on a short term basis.' She turned to Kesri. 'If I have your permission to take the time off.'

'By all means. The break will do you good. You've been working very long hours since you've been here. You know what they say about "all work and no play". You may find the desert inspires you.'

There were moments, in the desert, when Nicole suspected Alex of making their journey especially arduous. Dan loved every minute, but there were times when she had to grit her teeth and endure the long jolting drives between stops and the uncomfortable conditions when they did reach where they were going.

Determined not to betray by so much as the flicker of an eyelash that she longed to be back in the luxury of the palace, or even somewhere with fairly primitive mod cons, she forced herself to adapt to being hot, sticky, dirty and, much of the time, uncomfortable.

There was no way she could avoid looking a mess and the fact that Alex was unshaven and unwashed didn't make her feel any better. Several days' growth of stubble looked good on him and even the smell of his sweat was not offensive. Something deeply primitive in her responded to the sheen and scent of his hot tanned skin. But she felt he must find her increasingly unattractive as heat and dust took their toll.

He had an uncanny knack of picking her lowest moments to make a sardonic remark. Once, when she had been relieving herself behind the inadequate shelter of a thorn bush, praying not to encounter a snake or scorpion, he greeted her return with, 'The nightmare will soon be over.'

Nicole raised her eyebrows. 'What makes you think it's a nightmare?'

'Isn't it?'

'Not in the least…it's a fantastic adventure.'

And, in a way, it was. Despite the physical discomforts, despite her longing for a shower, she wasn't sorry she had come. If only for a little while, the three of them felt like a family. It gave her a sense of unity she had never previously experienced.

But perhaps from his perspective, having a woman and child with him was an encumbrance.

As their journey came to an end, Alex glanced at Nicole who was sitting beside him, gazing ahead at Karangarh which, from this angle and this distance, looked like one of the lost cities of legend.

He knew, although she denied it, that much of the trip had been an ordeal for her. But she had stood up to it well, never complaining about the primitive conditions. How much of her stoicism had been motivated by a desire not to spoil things for Dan, it was hard to tell.

Alex had half expected her to crumble when the reality of desert travel, uncushioned by tourist concessions, made itself felt. Instead, when her hair became lank, she had hidden it with a turban that drew his attention to the beauty of her forehead and cheekbones. If she minded having dirty feet and less than perfectly clean hands, she did not allow it to show. Nor did she wrinkle her nose when he was near her. For his part,

he found her natural aroma curiously erotic. If they had
been on their own, he would have found it hard to
restrain himself.

Even now, with the boy sitting behind them, he had
to control an urge to take one of her hands from her
lap and sink his teeth into the softness at the base of
her thumb. He wanted her more than he had on her
first night in India. She was becoming an obsession
which he would have to cure.

Although it was a long time since Dan had believed in
Father Christmas, he still enjoyed finding a football
sock stuffed with small presents on the end of his bed
on Christmas morning. The Christmas after his eighth
birthday, he had filled a stocking for Nicole. It had not
been his grandfather's idea. Dan had thought of it off
his own bat and continued it every year since.

This year, in place of the football sock, Nicole had
designed a drawstring bag and had it made up by one
of the craftspeople who were working on her other designs. She filled it with small inexpensive presents and
took it to Dan's room in the last hours of Christmas
Eve.

Early next morning she was woken by a rustling
sound close to her ear. It was Dan scrunching a handful
of wrapping paper, preparatory to announcing, with a
big grin, that Father Christmas had found out where
they were.

'Poor Granpa...imagine having to spend Christmas
in a hotel with lots of strangers,' he said, a little later,
through a mouthful of chocolate.

By this time they had opened their parcels and
Nicole's bed was strewn with small pieces of decorative paper.

'They'll enjoy it,' she said. 'When people get older it's better for them to have all the organising and cooking taken off their shoulders.'

Privately, she felt a pang at the thought of her father spending Christmas without anyone of his own blood to celebrate with him.

'When it's mid-morning there, we'll ring him,' she said cheerfully. 'If we can get through.'

Christmas Day was a public holiday throughout India but Karangarh was too far off the main tourist track to have been affected, as yet, by the spread of commercialised Christmas. Kesri had told Nicole that he wanted to keep those aspects at bay as long as possible.

Nevertheless she had felt that modest Christmas presents to him and to Alex would be appropriate. But what to give a maharaja and a man whose spiritual home was the desert had been a big problem. She could only hope that, when they met before dinner, the two men would like the way she had solved it.

'Were you able to get through to your grandfather?' Kesri asked Dan, when he and his mother joined the two men for private drinks before joining the guests in the hotel for the festive dinner laid on for them.

'Yes, thank you, sir. Merry Christmas, sir.' Dan presented his gift, an audiobook chosen by him and bought with his own money. He then produced a similar present for Alex.

Both men professed themselves delighted. Kesri's present to Dan was a length of multicoloured cotton intended for use as a turban. It was something Dan had wanted, although not as much as what Alex gave him.

His gasp of astonished pleasure made it clear that the CD he had just unwrapped was something special.

'It's a flight simulator, Mum. I've been dying for one for ages, and this is the best. Thanks, Alex.'

In a spontaneous gesture, he opened his arms and stepped forward, then stopped short and blushed with embarrassment.

It was clear to Nicole and, she thought, must be plain to the others that her son's instinctive reaction had been to give Alex the hug he would have given her father had the present been from him.

To cover his embarrassment, she said, 'Have you tried it out, Alex? Is it as close to flying as people say?'

'I haven't tested it, no. But I checked with a nephew who knows about these things. Perhaps when Dan's got the hang of it, he'll let us all have a go.'

He smiled at the boy in a way that made Nicole's heart ache for all that her son had missed by not having someone like Alex in his life since he was little.

Now it was time for her presents. Kesri gave her a pashmina shawl. Alex's parcel was larger and heavier, containing a lavishly illustrated book on the history, styles and patterns of the sari. She was overwhelmed by their generosity and had a deflating feeling that her presents to them would seem very meagre by comparison.

'I hope you'll make allowances for my deficiencies as a portraitist,' she said, offering them the two small packages.

What they contained had taken her a long time to do, but now she was not sure it had been a good idea. She had always been attracted by English portrait miniatures, the paintings on ovals of ivory which, in the time before photography, had served as mementoes of loved ones.

The portrait of Kesri she had given to Alex was painted on card, not ivory, but she thought she had caught a good likeness. The one of Alex she had felt curiously reluctant to part with.

'My dear Nicole, you are too modest, this is really excellent,' said Kesri. He looked at the portrait of himself that Alex was holding. 'I had no idea that we were both under your microscope. You must have remarkable powers of observation to have portrayed us so accurately, or were these painted from photographs you took without our knowledge?'

She shook her head. 'I have quite a good memory for people's features. And both you and Alex have very striking faces.'

Alex had still not reacted. She wished she could read his mind. Then he looked up.

'Thank you, Nicole. Anything made by hand is particularly welcome...unless it's a hideous sweater knitted with more enthusiasm than taste by an ancient great-aunt,' he added, with a smile. 'But this is not in that category.'

A few days later, Alex came to the studio while Nicole was working on some adaptations of folk designs she had copied during the trip.

'Can you take a break? There's something I want to discuss with you,' he said.

His tone and manner suggested it was something serious.

'Is it about Dan?' she asked, wondering what mischief her son could have perpetrated. So far his behaviour had been exemplary, but he wasn't an angel and couldn't be expected always to behave like one.

'No...at least not directly. But it would affect him,' said Alex. 'To come straight to the point, it's a proposal of marriage. I've come to ask you to marry me.'

'Marry you?' Nicole said faintly, unable to believe she could have heard him correctly.

'You sound astonished.'

'I am!'

'Why?' he asked bluntly.

'Well...because...because I didn't think you were interested in marrying anyone...least of all me.'

'Until recently I wasn't interested in marriage. Or, to be accurate, in marrying again. As you may know, I was married once...a long time ago.' His expression remained impassive as he went on, 'My wife was killed a few days after our first wedding anniversary. For years afterwards I blamed myself for putting her in the situation that led to her death. But no amount of remorse can alter the past. I've spent too long looking back. Now I have to look to the future. Your son needs a father. My father needs a grandson.' He paused for a moment. 'I think you and I both need the practical benefits of marriage. Companionship. Moral support. Someone to share our bed.'

'What about love? You haven't mentioned love.'

'I was in love with my wife. I take it that you were in love with Dan's father?'

'Yes.'

'Then we've both had that kind of young love. It makes more sense now to see love from the Indian perspective...as something that, hopefully, grows from living together and raising children together. You wouldn't object to having more children, would you?'

I would love to have your child, she thought. Aloud, she said, 'When Dan was small I wanted him to have siblings. But when it came to the point I couldn't marry for that reason only. I actually backed out of a relationship with someone who would have made Dan an excellent stepfather because—' She hesitated, afraid the stark truth might put him off her. Then, deciding this was no time for side-stepping, she went on, 'Because he was good and true as a person, but completely clueless as a lover. We went away for a weekend. After two nights I knew I couldn't spend the rest of my life—'

'Closing your eyes and thinking of England?' Alex cut in.

Relieved that he seemed amused, she nodded. 'Exactly.'

'Would you like to have a weekend somewhere with me before you commit yourself?'

She wasn't sure if he was serious or taking the mickey.

'Kesri might take it in his stride. I don't think Dan would.'

'I'm sure it could be arranged for him to be elsewhere while I gave you a demonstration of my capabilities.'

Refusing to rise to the bait, Nicole said calmly, 'You're making me think this whole thing is an elaborate tease.'

'I assure you it isn't. I was joking about the demo, but about a marriage between us I couldn't be more serious. It's been in my mind since our camping trip.'

'Perhaps you haven't thought hard enough. How would your father react to your marrying a woman with a child born outside marriage?'

'My father credits me with enough sense to choose a wife who will suit me.'

When he left it at that, she said, 'Don't you want to know how it happened?'

'If you want to tell me. Not if you don't. As I said, the past is behind us.'

'But I have a living reminder of what, in some people's eyes, is still a regrettable lapse if no longer a major disgrace.'

'"He that is without sin let him cast the first stone",' Alex said. 'Perhaps you had better tell me what happened. It obviously weighs on your mind.'

'Only in the context of marriage. If people thinking of marrying aren't straight with each other from the start, how can it work?'

'OK...fire away.'

Not sure where to begin, Nicole said, 'Dan's father, Pete, was the brother of a schoolfriend of mine. I wasn't the only one who fell for him. Most of my class were crazy about him. I don't know why he liked me best. We were chalk and cheese. Pete was into rock music, discos and smoking pot. I was into art books and design magazines. I suppose what kept us together was wanting each other. The urge to mate is so strong at that age. It makes everything else seem unimportant.'

'That's why, in India, it's taboo for girls and boys to spend time alone together,' Alex said dryly.

'Pete wanted us to make love, but I felt we shouldn't. I knew it would upset my father if he found out. He trusted me not to do things I'd been brought up to believe were wrong. Then Pete's father was promoted and they moved away. I missed Pete terribly. After weeks apart, he borrowed a car and drove over to see me. My father was out. We both got carried away. Pete said it would be all right, but it wasn't. When I told him I was pregnant, he dumped me. He didn't behave well, but basically it was my fault. I shouldn't have relied on him to make sure nothing went wrong. A woman's body is her own responsibility.'

'He behaved abominably,' Alex said, scowling. 'He was the child's father. To leave you to cope on your own was unforgivably cowardly.'

'It becomes more understandable when you know what else had just happened to him. The band he was with had just made a single. When a local disc jockey gave it air time, it was an instant hit…the million-to-one breakthrough that every band dreams of. There was no way Peter could fit a pregnant teenage wife into his life. His decision was hard on me, but it was the right one for him.'

'And where is he now? Stuck in some dead-end job or living on handouts?' Alex asked cuttingly.

Knowing the scorn in his tone was not aimed at her, she said, 'No, that's what usually happens, but in this case it didn't. He went on to fame and fortune, and it wasn't a flash in the pan. He's still a star, a big one. You wouldn't recognise his stage name because it's not your sort of music. But most rock fans would.'

'Does Dan know this?'

'He knows his father's real name. Not the rest of it. I'll tell him that when he's older…if he asks. He's never shown much curiosity about his father.'

'Isn't that unusual?'

'Why should he be interested in a father who isn't interested in him?'

'I thought children separated from their parents always were. Have you had any contact with his father?'

'When Dan was three, Pete wrote offering me money. I turned it down. He wrote again saying he had opened a bank account for Dan. He gave me the address of the bank and the account number. If I wanted to draw money from it, all I would have to do would be to produce identification. I don't know if it's still there...if he's still putting money in. If he is, it will be a nest-egg for Dan when he's older. If he's prepared to take money in lieu of love.'

'You have every right to hate Pete, but perhaps there's a part of you that still loves him,' said Alex. 'Women can be incredibly forgiving to men who treat them badly.'

'I know, but I'm not one of them. I've never hated Pete. But I certainly don't have a lingering yen for him. If you want the unvarnished truth, he made such a botch of my first time that I went off him there and then.'

'Perhaps it was his first time too,' Alex suggested.

Nicole shook her head. 'There had been other girls. He had quite a lot of experience, but no understanding of women. He didn't even try to make it nice for me. Once you realise that, you fall out of love pretty fast.''

'Have all your lovers been bunglers?'

'I've only had three. Considering my age, that isn't exactly wild living.'

'How did the third rate?'

'We had other problems. He was active politically and I find politics boring. He wanted me to learn to play golf. He hadn't read a book—not even an airport novel—since he left school. We decided it wasn't going to work.'

'But it was all right in bed?'

She decided to temper the truth. If she admitted it

had not been all right, he would be sure to conclude there was something wrong with her. He might withdraw his proposal.

'Yes, it was fine,' she said.

'Thank God for that,' said Alex. 'Three bunglers in succession would have put you off men for life. I've always felt sorry for women in that respect. It seems unfair that your pleasure mechanisms are more complicated than ours. Are you sure you can take it on trust that I won't be a bungler?'

'I knew that you weren't a selfish man when you backed off the night I arrived.'

'There was nothing else I could do.'

'You could have kissed me again. My resistance wasn't very strong. You could easily have…overwhelmed me. I'm sure you knew that.'

'It seemed possible,' he agreed. 'Perhaps instinct told me to wait…that delaying might work out better. As it has. You are going to marry me, aren't you?'

Nicole drew a deep breath. Even with love on both sides, it was such a momentous commitment. With love on only one side, it was even more scary.

'Yes,' she said firmly. 'Yes.'

'Then shall we seal the agreement in the conventional way?' He opened his hands, his fingers beckoning her closer.

She took a step towards him, her heartbeat starting to accelerate. His hands settled on her waist. He closed the gap between them, looking into her eyes until the intensity of his gaze made her close them. His lips brushed her temple and cheekbone, moving lightly down to the corner of her mouth and pausing there for several tantalising seconds before taking possession of her lips.

But he didn't let the kiss blow their minds the way it had last time. Before it got to that stage, he raised his head and relaxed his hold.

'Let's get married here...right away.'

'Can we do that?'

'Why not? People get married away from wherever they come from all the time. Kesri's secretary will sort out the formalities for us. All you have to do is decide what you're going to wear. It won't be a formal occasion but I expect you'll want a new dress.'

She wondered what his first wedding had been like. Had the girl called Nuala worn white? Had it been a big family wedding with women in wide-brimmed hats and men in morning dress?

She couldn't ask. Not now...probably never. It was a part of his life that would always be fenced off and private.

When she told Dan, he was thrilled.

'That's brilliant, Mum. It's what I was hoping would happen, but somehow I got the feeling you weren't very keen on Alex.'

'Really? I can't think why. He's everything I admire.'

'Won't Granpa be surprised? When are you going to ring him?'

'I'd better do that right away. I don't think he's up to coming here for the wedding. That long flight would be too exhausting.'

'And if he came, *she* would come too, and that would spoil it,' said her son.

'"She" isn't polite. Say Rosemary,' Nicole reproved him, while inwardly agreeing that her stepmother's presence would cast a blight on the occasion. Her airs and graces wouldn't cut any ice with Alex and

Kesri. They would both detest her, though their impeccable manners would forbid them to show it.

It took some time to get a call through to her father. She wished they had an email link. But Rosemary was suspicious of the Internet and had encouraged him in his mistaken belief that he was too old to cope with it.

It was Rosemary who answered the telephone, insisting on telling Nicole a lot of local gossip she had no desire to hear before finally passing the receiver to her husband.

After asking him how he was, Nicole said, 'Dad, do you remember finding that newspaper cutting about Dr Alex Strathallen, the man who interviewed me for this job?'

When her father replied that he did, she said, 'Well, this will come as a surprise, because I haven't mentioned him much in my letters to you, but he's asked me to marry him and I've said yes. Dan is over the moon. I'll hope you'll be pleased for us too. When you meet Alex, I know you're going to like him.'

'If you like him, so shall I. This is wonderful news,' said her father.

After they had said goodbye, Nicole wondered if Rosemary would share his enthusiasm. Most women in her position would have been pleased at the thought of having their husband and their house to themselves. But with her stepdaughter and her husband's grandson gone, Rosemary would have only one person to harry and that might not suit her as well as having three.

The following day while Dan was out somewhere with Alex, Kesri came to the studio.

'Alex has told me your news. I'm delighted. You are very well-suited.'

'Are we? How do you know?'

'Alex and I are like brothers. I've known you a much shorter time, but the way you have brought up your son is proof that you'll be a good wife. It's not easy for a woman to raise a boy on her own. Too often she becomes over-protective and over-possessive. You've avoided those pitfalls. Dan is a splendid chap. I don't think you need to worry that he'll be jealous when you have children with Alex. He's past the age when noses get put out of joint.'

'I hope so,' said Nicole.

This was something she had thought about during a wakeful night. Lying in bed, unable to sleep, she wondered if a marriage made for 'practical benefits' could ever lead to the kind of marriage she had always hoped for. That practical marriages appeared to work in India, and had once been common in the western world, didn't allay her misgivings. Nor did the fact that everyone who knew about Alex and herself seemed in favour of their alliance.

She wondered if Kesri had mentioned it to his sister yet and hated the thought of Chandra being heartbroken. In many ways she and Alex seemed ideally matched...unless, despite his close friendship with Alex, Kesri would not wish to have him for a brother-in-law and Alex knew that.

The next time they were alone, she said, 'Alex, do you realise that Chandra's regard for you goes much deeper than a sisterly affection?'

He didn't look surprised by her question. 'I know how Chandra feels, but I don't return those feelings. Even if I had been fond of her in that way, it couldn't have worked. In her heart of hearts, she knows this. Chandra has made a commitment to spend the rest of her life improving the lot of less privileged women. She'll never leave India. Sooner or later I must give up my freedom and go back to Scotland to take on my father's responsibilities. You do understand what lies ahead of you, don't you? One of these days you're going to have to share that future with me?'

'If you think I'm capable of doing whatever it involves.'

'In the past, when a woman's primary function was being a wife and mother, Strathallen wives were more involved than they will be in the future. You're a professional designer. I wouldn't ask you to give up your career. I'm sure you'd refuse anyway. All you will have to do is make yourself pleasant at a few social occasions and give birth to however many children we decide to have.'

One of her troubling night-thoughts came into her mind. 'What if I can't produce any children? Have you considered that?'

'Was Dan's birth difficult? Were you advised against having more children?'

She shook her head. 'His birth was very easy. But sometimes women of my age have a problem conceiving.'

Unexpectedly, he put out his hand and stroked her cheek with the backs of his fingers. 'You talk as if your biological clock was striking the eleventh hour. You're only just in your thirties. You have plenty of time to have two or three more children...and our income will allow you to have plenty of help with the nursery chores.'

'I wouldn't want to hand over my...our babies to

other people. I'd put my career on hold while they were little, or at least reduce my commitments.'

'That's up to you. I wouldn't press you to do it. I hope to keep my own work going even after I have to go back to Scotland. Though, once that happens, I won't be able to come to India much.'

'*Must* you take over from your father? Is your sense of duty so strong that you wouldn't be able to live with yourself if you didn't?'

'I've thought about that a lot. Should anyone have their life, or even a part of it, mapped out for them in advance? At the highest level, should the heirs to thrones have to accept being crowned if they don't want to be? With Princely India now history, must Kesri accept all the burdens that go with his privileges? At a much lower level, must I? It's certainly not my choice to spend the last half of my life in a draughty castle in an unfriendly climate. But is it my duty? What do you think?'

She knew that he wasn't really asking her opinion. His decision was already made. He just wanted to see what she would say.

'How can I possibly answer that? I come from a long line of people whose lives are forgotten in two or three generations. My only family heirloom is my mother's grandmother's locket. So I don't have a clue how I'd feel if I were in your or Kesri's shoes. I can see that your father might want you to follow him and, if you'd given him your word, you wouldn't want to go back on it.'

'You've got it in one,' said Alex. 'When it all seemed too far ahead to be real, I promised my father I'd hold the estate together for my son. Now that eventuality isn't as remote as it was in my early twenties.'

'But if your father is in good health, it's still a long way off. You might die before he does.' Even to suggest the possibility sent a shiver of anguish through her.

Now that she loved him, how could she bear a world where he had ceased to exist? 'I think we should live in the present and let the future take care of itself. But whatever happens, if I'm your wife, I'll go wherever you have to go.'

'There's no ''if'' about it. It's settled. You *are* going to be my wife,' he said, taking her in his arms. 'But I don't think fundamentalist feminists would approve of you being ready to pack up and follow wherever I lead.'

'I don't need their approval. I have my own convictions. Two women I was at school with have split with their partners because their careers were pulling in different directions. If I knew what had happened to the rest of the class, there are probably more in that situation. But even top jobs aren't secure any more. The only real security is a strong…relationship.' She had almost said 'strong and loving' but managed to clip off the words that were inappropriate, hoping he hadn't noticed the brief hiatus.

But Alex's thoughts had changed direction. 'Stop talking and kiss me,' he commanded.

Nicole was happy to comply but no sooner had she raised her lips than there was the sound of whistling and moments later Dan's voice calling, 'Mum, are you here?' from the lobby.

Chandra didn't come to the wedding because, so she wrote, it clashed with an unbreakable speaking engagement. But she sent them an exquisite wedding present: an Indian miniature painting of lovers resting under a tree by the edge of a lake fringed with lotus flowers. With it was a note, which Nicole felt sure was sincere, wishing them a lifetime of happiness.

Nicole woke up on her wedding day determined not to allow her private misgivings to cloud what should be one of the happiest days of her life.

So far, her happiest days had been her graduation from art school and the day she first saw Dan. Because of the circumstances, she had been afraid she might find it hard if not impossible to love him. But when they had given him to her, with his eyes tightly shut and his tiny mouth pursed in furious resentment at being forced out of his previous and much cosier environment, she had felt a surge of protectiveness.

To her relief he hadn't looked at all like his father. For by then her infatuation had died and she knew how stupid she had been to let it overrule her common sense. It had never been love that she felt. Like numerous other silly girls she had been swept away by a teenage crush and, without her father's support, it could have wrecked her life.

Dan came to her room while she was putting on her make-up. It had been decided the wedding would be extremely informal with the bridegroom and his prospective step-son wearing open-necked shirts and chinos. Dan's blue shirt and pale beige trousers had been made for him by a Karangarh tailor.

'Hi, Mum. How are you feeling? Nervous?' he asked.

'Not specially. You're looking nice. Do you like my outfit?' She gestured to where it was hanging.

After several changes of mind, she had settled for a version of the *salwar kameez* she had admired in the garden at the Imperial on her first day in Delhi. Both

the long tunic and loose trousers were made from
printed silk in shades of hot pink and deep red that
might look garish in Europe but vibrated beautifully
together in the strong light of Rajasthan.

'I didn't know brides wore red.'

'They do in India. Wonderful red and gold saris.'

'Oh, help, I almost forgot. This is for you...from
Alex.' Dan fished in his pocket and brought out a small
flat velvet-covered box. 'He gave it to me last night.'

CHAPTER SEVEN

NICOLE had not expected a present and had nothing to give in return. The case contained a pair of flamboyant gold and ruby earrings. She knew that the city of Jaipur, the capital of Rajasthan, was famous for the cutting and polishing of gemstones, but had not known that work of this quality was to be found in Karangarh. The earrings were perfect with her outfit, much more exciting than the plain gold hoops she had planned to wear.

Dan stayed until she was ready and it was time to make their way to the hotel part of the palace and the room where both the formalities and the wedding lunch were being held.

At the entrance to the hotel they were met by two of the palace staff who carefully lifted a garland of jasmine over Nicole's head and adorned her son with a garland of golden marigolds.

Kesri and Alex, who were waiting for them in the bridal chamber, were also wearing garlands.

The registrar who was to conduct the ceremony had already arrived. After the introductions, everyone took their places and in a very short time the official part of the occasion was over and she was a married woman being photographed with her husband.

It wasn't until champagne was being served that she was able to thank Alex for the earrings.

'I had a hunch you might decide to follow the custom of the country and wear red today. It suits you. You look gorgeous,' he told her, smiling.

'Thank you.' She wondered if he meant it or was merely playing his part.

When they had eaten lunch, Kesri made a short speech wishing them health and happiness.

'Now, in conclusion, I have a surprise for you,' he said. 'You thought you were spending your wedding night in the *haveli* that we finished restoring last month. But we have arranged something even more romantic for you...the first of our Desert Honeymoons. Alex knows the desert and its inhabitants as well as anyone. In the short time she has been here, Nicole has been quick to understand how the traditions of our past can be adapted to the future. It seems highly appropriate that these two people should be the ones to "test drive" this exciting innovation.'

Nicole smiled and tried to looked pleased, while inwardly feeling that their honeymoon might be testing enough without the guinea pig element.

The *haveli* Kesri had mentioned was one of the many houses built by affluent merchants in Karangarh's heyday. Its restoration complete, it was going to house the new tourist office with two luxury apartments above, in one of which they had been going to spend the first forty-eight hours of their new life together.

She also felt that a wedding trip in the desert would make Dan feel more left out. But it turned out that Kesri had another surprise up his sleeve. Immediately after the wedding, he was flying to Jaisalmer, another of Rajasthan's fortress-cities, and taking Dan with him.

'Did you know about the change of plan?' she asked Alex, after they had waved goodbye to his friend and her son as they left for the airstrip.

'I knew about Jaisalmer, not about the "test drive". But it's typical of Kesri. Once he gets an idea in his head, he can't wait to see it in action.' He tucked her hand through his arm to stroll back across the huge courtyard and into the palace. 'He'll expect a written report, you know. You'll have to make careful notes.'

It was said with a poker face but she knew he was teasing and laughed. 'How far will we have to drive? I'd better change into something more suitable.'

'While you're doing that, I'll check out the details. I wouldn't expect the location to be too far away because of the logistics. I'll come and pick you up as soon as I know the arrangements.' Taking her hand from his arm, he raised it to his lips and kissed it before taking off in a different direction from the route to her quarters.

Nicole had already packed what she would need for a couple of nights in the *haveli*. She had been planning to stay in her wedding outfit for the rest of the day, but now she changed into combat trousers and a T-shirt.

When Alex joined her, he said, 'As I thought, it's not far as the crow flies but Kesri has devised a route that will make the honeymooners who follow us feel they're a lot further from civilisation than they actually are. Are you ready to go?'

Normally Nicole had a good sense of direction. But once they were out of sight of Karangarh, she found it hard to keep her bearings as they followed a series of rough tracks across arid wasteland and, later, among barren dunes that all looked alike to her.

She wondered what they would find when they reached their destination and how many people had been assigned to look after them. She wondered if Alex would wait until tonight to make love to her. Or if he would want to retire to their sleeping quarters soon after they arrived.

What activities did a desert honeymoon offer other than making love? Reading? Going for walks among the dunes? Maybe, for a couple who were mad about each other, Kesri's brainchild was a great idea. But in this particular marriage, where the madness was all on one side, suddenly a desert seemed the most unsuitable location imaginable.

'You've gone very quiet,' said Alex, taking his eyes off the track for a few seconds to give her a searching glance.

Rather than share her inappropriate thoughts, she told him something that had been in her mind soon after waking that morning.

'I was thinking that if, six months ago, a fortune teller had predicted a tall dark stranger, a journey to a far country and a wedding, I'd have dismissed it as impossible nonsense.'

'The journey might have seemed far-fetched. I don't know why you would have thought the stranger and the wedding nonsensical. What surprises me is that you haven't been snapped up before,' he said, with a smiling look.

It was a pleasant thing to hear, but she couldn't help wondering if he meant it or was just being nice to her.

Before she could think of a suitable reply, their destination came into view. A magnificent tent, almost large enough to accommodate an English wedding reception or a country house auction, had been erected in a valley in the dunes.

'That's a relic of the days of the *shikars*…the great tiger hunts,' said Alex, as they approached it. 'In Kesri's grandfather's time, VIPS visiting Rajasthan would be invited to shoot blackbuck from the back of an open Rolls-Royce speeding across the desert at fifty miles an hour. It seems strange to us now that people would want to kill wild animals. But it wasn't the *shikars* that nearly wiped out the tiger. It was the destruction of their habitats. So you needn't have scruples about sleeping under the canvas that sheltered the trophy hunters.'

The suggestion was so far removed from what *was* on her mind that she almost laughed.

'I don't,' she said candidly. 'They lived in a different age and had different outlooks. When Kesri was showing me round, soon after I arrived, he told me a few of the hotel visitors didn't approve of the stuffed tigers around the palace until he pointed out they were historic relics like the handprints of the women who sacrificed themselves on their husbands' funeral pyres. I've forgotten the date he said that custom was banned.'

'About a hundred and seventy years ago. I hate seeing those little handprints on palace walls,' Alex said, frowning. 'We're all bound by custom in some way, but I can't understand how men with power and influence, if they cared for their wives, could allow that custom to continue.'

Nicole wished she hadn't mentioned the subject. Perhaps, for Alex, the handprints left by the women who had died in that way might evoke painful personal memories of his first wife's death.

Today, of all days, she did not want to think about the girl he had married for love, or to feel that he was remembering Nuala. Yet logic told her that thoughts of his first wife must have been in his mind from the moment he woke. How could they not have been?

Inevitably, certain occasions triggered memories of similar occasions. She herself had been reminded of friends' weddings. How could he have closed his mind to his own first wedding day?

As they neared the great tent, two of the palace staff came out of the canopied entrance. By the time Alex stopped the Jeep, they were waiting with welcoming smiles to deal with the small amount of luggage.

The interior of the tent encompassed more than one room, the one immediately inside the doorway being arranged and furnished as a sitting room with comfortable chairs, small tables and even a writing table. On top of a pegged-taut canvas flooring, several beautiful rugs had been spread.

'Let's have tea outside, shall we?' said Alex.

In what Nicole could now recognise as Marwari, the dialect of Rajasthani spoken in Karangarh, he had a conversation with a third man who had appeared.

Afterwards, he said to Nicole, 'If you'd like to wash your hands, you'll find an ablutions tent for your exclusive use in that direction. Mine is the other way.'

While he waited for her to return from exploring the washing facilities, Alex wished he had arranged to spend the first few days of their marriage in the palace hotel on the lake at Udaipur where, although it was always busy during the tourist season, they would, in some ways, have had greater privacy.

Much as he loved the desert, it was not the place he would have chosen to spend these first hours with Nicole. They would have to wait until after dinner and the servants had retired to the service tent in another part of the dunes before they would be really alone.

The reason he had not arranged to go to Udaipur,

perhaps the most romantic place in the whole of Rajasthan, was because he had been there before with Nuala. There were not many places in this part of India they hadn't visited together. They had even camped in the desert, but not at this level of luxury. Their only attendant had been a drunken camel-driver who, as they travelled on foot, had followed behind with their gear. In the mornings they had woken drenched by the condensation from their own body heat during cold desert nights in sleeping bags.

But that was a long time ago and better forgotten, which was why he had decided an apartment in the *haveli* was the best location for starting this new phase of life. Then, with the best intentions, Kesri had scotched that plan and here they were, stuck in a situation that was plainly accentuating Nicole's first-night nerves.

Why, at her age, with plenty of evidence that they would be good together, she was palpably jumpy, he wasn't sure. It must have something to do with her previous experiences. It annoyed him to think of anyone treating her badly, even if only from thoughtlessness. Despite her professional assurance, in most other respects she seemed to him curiously vulnerable.

Nicole came round the corner of the big tent and saw Alex with his arms folded and an expression she could only describe as grim hardening his strongly marked features. It disturbed her that, thinking himself unobserved, he looked anything but happy. Though the grim look vanished when he saw her, she had an uneasy feeling he might already be regretting this precipitate marriage.

She debated asking him point-blank what was on his

mind. But she doubted if he would tell her. It seemed best to behave as if she hadn't noticed him looking like the dour Scot of popular myth.

'The people who come here after us won't be able to find fault with the washing facilities. Considering where we are, they're amazing,' she said brightly.

'Good, I'm glad you approve,' said Alex.

It seemed to her that, far from being that of an impatient bridegroom, his tone sounded more like a seasoned traveller on the first night of one of the package tours she had been on with her father. Polite but slightly wary of being trapped by the tour bore.

Wondering how they were going to get through the hours till bedtime, she was relieved when a small procession appeared and began the ritual of serving afternoon tea.

Tea was followed by drinks while watching the sun set. Then more drinks were served while they listened to old-fashioned records played on a wind-up gramophone that Kesri thought would amuse the sophisticated clientele he hoped would enjoy a return to the pleasures of the past.

They ate their dinner by candlelight, discussing the books they had read as children and teenagers. It wasn't a strained conversation, but nor was it wholly relaxed, at least not on her side.

Alex ate his food slowly, savouring the subtle flavours of the dishes served to them on a *thali*, a round silver tray with various smaller containers arranged round its edge. Crested silver forks and spoons had been provided and they used them.

'The best way to eat Indian food is with the fingers,' he said. 'Using cutlery is like drinking wine from a mug or through a straw. It doesn't taste the same as it does from a wine glass. Some westerners aren't comfortable eating moist food with their fingers. It's a far more sensual experience and that makes them uneasy.'

'Perhaps they were told off as children for having sticky fingers.'

'You could be right. Most hang-ups do start that way. One of my sisters liked running around with bare feet. Then someone we had staying with us put it into her head that the heather was alive with snakes. There are snakes in that kind of terrain, but the risk of treading on an adder is minimal. But once a fear is implanted, it's hard to get rid of it.'

'I know. My mother was afraid of spiders and I've inherited that. But when Dan was little I made a big effort to control my revulsion so that he wouldn't pick it up. Do you have any hang-ups, Alex?'

'I'm not keen on caving. I've tried it a couple of times and was glad to get back above ground.'

She liked him for admitting to something he could have kept quiet about.

'You are rather big for squirming through narrow tunnels. I wouldn't like the dark and the danger of getting stuck. One of the masters at Marsden is mad keen on speleology. I'm praying he doesn't make Dan want to try it. I don't want to hold him back from anything he wants to do, but the thought of him trapped somewhere in the bowels of the earth...'

She gave an expressive shiver, at the same time wondering if it was tactless to keep bringing her son into the conversation when, tonight of all nights, her mind should be focussed on her husband.

'I shouldn't worry about it. At the moment he's set

his sights on learning to fly. That wouldn't worry you, would it?'

'Not at all. Flying, gliding, para-gliding...all those things seem more natural than burrowing under the earth.'

After dinner, coffee was served. At last the servants withdrew and they were really alone.

'More music?' Alex asked.

'Fine by me,' she agreed.

Instead of winding up the gramophone, he went to another section of the tent and came back with a transistor radio and a tape. As soon as it began to play, she recognised it as a favourite tape she had had to leave behind in England.

'I have this too,' she said, smiling.

'Two unashamed middlebrows...that seems a good augury.'

By the time the tape finished, they had also used up all the coffee.

'The showpiece of the desert is the sunrise,' said Alex. 'If we're going to be up in time to see it, perhaps we should call it a day.'

'I'll go and brush my teeth.' Nicole knew that her nightgown and robe had already been draped over a chair in the ablutions tent by whoever had unpacked her belongings.

In her early days at Karangarh, she had found it strange to have someone else handling her most personal belongings, but now she was accustomed to it. It wouldn't have surprised her if Tara had been among their entourage, but it seemed that all their attendants were men.

A large vacuum jug was now by the basin on the washstand. She did not have to wash in cold water.

When she returned to the main tent, Alex was there before her. He was also wearing a robe of dark blue silk but without, she guessed, anything underneath it. There was a vee of bare chest showing between the lapels of the robe and his ankles were bare. On his feet he was wearing leather *jootis*, the decorative slippers worn by many Rajasthani men.

As she entered, he moved to the entrance to the inner tent and drew the flap aside. Feeling uncharacteristically nervous and shy, she moved past him into their bedroom.

Kesri had told her that, to attract and satisfy the richer tourists, it was necessary to provide a high degree of comfort with good camp beds and washing facilities that were not going to offend the most fastidious tourists.

Normally the sleeping tents were doubles equipped with twin beds. But in this tent a large divan had been prepared. It looked as if it were made from three single mattresses laid alongside each other and covered with specially woven sheets and an extra-large custom-made quilt.

Uncertain what to do, she stood with clasped hands looking at the thick candles inside glass shades that gave off a soft glow from the low tables placed on either side of the divan.

'It's been a long day. I expect what you'd really like is to curl up and go to sleep,' Alex said quietly.

He had closed the flap and was standing with his hands thrust into the two patch pockets on the front of his robe.

The truthful answer would have been, 'Yes, I would.'

But how could she say that to him?

She was his wife now. Even if the western world had moved on since the days when people talked about a husband's 'rights', the fact remained that men on their wedding night expected their brides to be willing participants in the pleasures of the nuptial bed.

Alex moved to where she was standing. Withdrawing his hands from his pockets, he placed them lightly on her shoulders. 'Let's try to be honest and open with each other, Nicole. This isn't an ordinary marriage. We've played the parts required of us in public. It's up to us how we deal with our private life. There are no rules, no "musts". Let's ignore the conventions and follow our instincts. My instinct tells me you need to relax and rest. So let's both do that, shall we?'

Taking her by the hand, he led her to one side of the bed where he stooped to turn back the covers. As if she were a child, he unfastened the sash of her robe, then moved round behind her to peel it back from her shoulders. When her arms were free of the sleeves, he said, 'Hop in. The sheets won't be cold. There are old-fashioned metal hot-water bottles between them.'

While she was climbing in, he put her robe over a camp chair before removing the shade from the candle and pinching out the flame between his finger and thumb.

Unable to believe he was willing to forego what usually happened on a wedding night, Nicole pulled the covers up to her chin and watched him walk round the divan to the other side. As he unfastened his own robe, she averted her eyes.

He got into bed before he extinguished the candle on his side of the bed. Then the tent was plunged into total darkness.

With her lying close to one side and him on the other, there was quite a large area of no man's land between them.

'Goodnight, my dear. Sleep well.'

'Goodnight.'

Perversely, now that she had been let off the hook, she felt disappointed, even resentful. All he had done by postponing their first congress was to prolong the tension. *Goodnight, my dear.* How middle-aged it sounded. The sort of thing men of her father's age said to wives for whom sex was a duty, not a delight.

She wondered how he would react if she were to take off her nightdress, wriggle across the empty territory between them and snuggle invitingly against him. But she didn't have the courage to find out. Which, for a woman of her age who had some experience, if not much, was ridiculous. If you could believe all you read, there were girls still in their teens who would deal with this situation without turning a hair. So why was she in such a dither about it?

Some time in the night, she woke up to find that while she had been sleeping the situation had changed. There was now an arm round her waist and her back was in close contact with a warm male chest.

It felt good. It felt very good. But how had it come about? Had he wrapped himself round her knowingly? Or could he have done it in his sleep? The latter didn't seem likely, considering how much space had separated them earlier.

As she lay considering the situation, there was a movement behind her. He lifted his head from the pillow and she felt his mouth touching the top of her shoulder, placing a row of feather-light kisses along it.

Nicole stayed very still, feigning sleep, which was hard to do while her heart was beginning to pound. Did he know she was awake? Or was he hoping to wake her?

He retraced the row of kisses, moving in the direction of her neck. At the same time, the arm round her waist drew back so that his hand was no longer resting somewhere on the bed in front of her but was beginning to explore her midriff. Instinctively Nicole tightened her tummy muscles and was glad she had when his hand strayed down past her navel and gently caressed the area between her hipbones.

She waited, her breathing arrested, for the exploration of her body to continue in a downwards direction. Instead of which it changed course and moved upwards.

As she often did, she had been sleeping with one hand under the pillow and her uppermost arm crossing her chest with the hand hooked round the outer end of her shoulder. This made it easy for his hand to make a leisurely reconnaissance of the soft curves of her breasts. Which in turn made it harder for her to lie motionless and keep her breathing steady.

His mouth was moving up the side of her neck now. When it reached the sensitive place behind her ear, she knew she couldn't pretend to be sleeping any longer. It was time to go through the motions of waking up. Slowly she straightened her legs and made a slight flexing movement of her shoulders.

The warm mouth moved to her nape and lingered there, sending slow ripples of pleasure down her spine.

Gently but firmly Alex turned her onto her back.

'I don't think you need a nightdress now you have

me to keep you warm,' he said, in a husky murmur, starting to remove it.

Nicole lifted her hips and then her shoulders, raising her arms above her head as he gathered the gossamer fabric and, when it was free, tossed it into the darkness. Then, for the first time, they were naked in each other's arms.

In reality it was a hundred times more exciting than in her imagination. She clung to him, parting her lips when she felt the touch of his mouth, pressing herself against him, wanting to make him feel welcome. There was no point in holding back now. Even if he didn't want her heart, at least she could be generous with her body.

When Nicole woke up it was light. She hadn't noticed last night, but the inner tent had two 'windows' which now had their flaps tied back to let in the early sunlight. The openings were still covered by insect-proof netting but it was too fine to obscure her view of the sunrise filling the sky with opalescent colours.

She slid out of bed and reached for her robe. She felt a different person from the woman who had woken yesterday. What had happened during the night had been a revelation. Yesterday she would not have believed that a man could be so tender, so patient, so determined to defer his pleasure until he had made sure of hers.

The experience had been totally unlike her initiation. Then, although she had been, or thought herself, madly in love with Dan's father, making love had been a traumatic disappointment. It had hurt. It had left her wondering what all the fuss was about. It had also made her pregnant. With convincing worldliness, Pete had said he would take care of things. But he hadn't.

This time the issue hadn't arisen. Alex wanted children and so did she. But, ironically, it was unlikely they had started a baby last night. It was the wrong time of her cycle.

Outside the tent's main entrance, on a rug spread under the canopy, two chairs had been placed on either side of a table. Here Alex was drinking tea and watching the sky change.

He rose to his feet when she joined him and said a smiling, 'Good morning. You're up early. I thought you would sleep late.'

'On my first day in the desert? I wish you had called me earlier. I wanted to see the whole sunrise...not just the last of it.'

'It will happen again tomorrow. Would you like some tea? They've only just brought it to me. Breakfast will come in about half an hour.'

'I'd love a cup. But first I must brush my teeth. You've already shaved, I see.'

He ran a hand over his jaw. 'I didn't think you'd go for a scratchy chin.'

When she returned with her face washed and her hair combed, he filled the other cup for her. 'So tell me, Mrs Strathallen, how did you find your first night in the desert?'

The gleam of amusement in his eyes and the memory of all that had happened in the darkness of the inner tent brought a flood of colour to her cheeks.

'It was...amazing.'

'I'm not sure if that's good or bad.'

She looked him straight in the eye. 'It was all and more than I hoped for. But I know I have a lot to learn about pleasing you. I'm not as *au fait* with these things as most women of my age. I haven't had a lot of practice.'

The next night, after their meal, Alex suggested a walk.

It was a bright moonlit night. Even the patterns left by the wind on the dunes were visible.

When they were out of sight of the camp, she said, 'The stars are brighter than I've ever seen them. I suppose that's because there's no light pollution. It seems a shame that children growing up in cities will never see stars as clearly as we can tonight.'

'You'll get a crick in your neck. Try star-gazing lying down.'

They were walking on hard stony ground but nearby were some dunes. Taking her hand, he led her towards them. Near the foot of a long slope of sand, he took off his fleece and spread it for her.

'Alex, you'll freeze,' she objected.

At night the temperature dropped. She had her fleece zipped up though he had been wearing his open.

'Not for five minutes, I won't.' He lowered himself to the sand, pulling her down beside him.

It *was* a marvellous experience, lying with her head resting comfortably on his shoulder and uncountable near and distant stars shimmering in the mysterious vastness of the night sky.

'I don't know why I can't get excited about space travel. Dan is longing to go. I suppose you are too,' she murmured, the stillness making a lowered voice seem appropriate.

'Not particularly. Dan is a child of the Space Age. Given the choice of an age to be born in, I've have preferred the pre-industrialised world.' He paused. 'Right now the only thing that excites me is you.'

Suddenly the night sky was blotted out by the shape of his head above hers. 'I want you,' he whispered fiercely against her mouth.

She knew that he meant here and now. For a second or two she was shocked, but also excited. There was something wild and primitive about making love in the open under the stars.

She put her arms round him. 'Then take me. I'm all yours.'

Afterwards, as they walked back, it seemed like something she had dreamed. Could she really have made love in that urgent, almost savage way with a man who found her desirable but didn't pretend to love her? And how long would their mutual lust last when, on his side, there were no deeper feelings to support it?

Later, when they went to bed, Alex left the candle alight on his side of the bed. Lying on his back with one hand under his head, he searched for and found her hand.

'Your appearance is deceptive. You look cool and self-contained. I always suspected you weren't. Are you tired now?'

'Not very.' She tried not to smile. 'Why do you ask?'

'Because I'd like you to show me how much you know about making love to a man. What you don't know, I'll teach you.'

They returned from their brief time alone together to find that Kesri had been at pains to keep Dan happily occupied. As well as the trip to Jaisalmer, he had started teaching the boy to ride and in the evening they had watched movies together.

Far from feeling left out, Dan had obviously had a great time and wouldn't have minded if they had stayed away longer.

But as the days passed and his time at Karangarh began to run out, it was clear he wasn't looking forward to returning to England and school.

'Couldn't I go to school here? Do I have to go back?' he asked Nicole, in Alex's hearing.

'I'm afraid you must, Dan,' she said. 'Granpa has made a lot of sacrifices for you to go to Marsden. He'd be terribly disappointed if we took you away. Besides, it wouldn't be easy to get you a place in a school here, and the syllabus would be different.'

'So what?' Dan said, scowling.

He caught Alex's eye, coloured and muttered, 'Sorry.'

Nicole put an arm round his shoulders. 'I understand how you feel but you'll be here again at Easter, and I'm sure once you're back you'll soon settle down.'

Later, alone with Alex, she said, 'I'm impressed by your ability to quell Dan with a look. Compared with some boys of his age, he's not often difficult.'

'He's very good-tempered,' said Alex. 'Don't worry: I shan't be a heavy-handed stepfather. But I'm not going to let it pass if he's rude to you. Perhaps he'd feel better about going back if we all went.'

'All of us? But I haven't been here long enough to ask for a break.'

'I'll ask for it on your behalf. Kesri won't object if I tell him I want to present you to my parents.'

'I think you should have done that *before* you married me,' she said, frowning slightly. 'I'm sure they must think it strange...our marrying in such a hurry.'

Alex took her face between his hands. 'I couldn't wait to have you.' His eyes were dark with desire as he slid his long fingers into the depths of her hair, cupping her head and bending his own to give her a hungry kiss as if he still couldn't wait.

'Would you have come to my bed before we were married?' he murmured against her cheek.

'I don't know. You didn't ask me.'

'Now I don't have to ask. I only have to do this...' As he spoke he unbuttoned her shirt, pushing it off her shoulders before doing the same with the thin satin straps of her bra.

Within seconds she was naked to the waist and he was caressing her breasts with his hands and lips.

Nicole closed her eyes and surrendered to warm waves of pleasure. She could not deny that, as long as they were somewhere private, he could do whatever he wanted and it would be what she wanted too. There was no way she could resist him.

But later when, passion spent, they were on the borders of sleep, her drowsiness was dispelled by the sudden realisation that his impatience to possess her might not be because he found her irresistible, but because, before their wedding night, he had not had a woman for a considerable time.

Seen in that light, his eagerness seemed less romantic.

CHAPTER EIGHT

WHEN their flight landed in Scotland, they were being met by his parents whose titles, Alex had explained, were The Strathallen of Strathallen and Madam Strathallen.

'There's no need to be nervous. They're very laid-back,' he assured her.

But although she had the confidence of a successful career to support her in most situations, in the one about to take place Nicole was acutely conscious that her background and his were poles apart. Which wasn't important to Alex, but was to his parents' generation, whose outlook had been formed in an era very different from today.

Had she arrived on her own, she would have had no difficulty in recognising her in-laws. Father and son were remarkably alike in their height, build and upright bearing. The Strathallen's hair was grey verging on white, but still as thick as his son's.

Madam Strathallen was also tall and grey-haired. It was she whom Alex embraced while Nicole and Dan stood back and watched them exchange hearty hugs. At least they were not an undemonstrative family, she thought, as he hugged his father.

Then he turned to present her to them. 'This is my wife, Nicole, and my stepson, Dan.'

'We've been so looking forward to this.' Smiling warmly, her mother-in-law shook hands with Nicole.

'Hello, Dan.' She gave him her hand. Then her husband shook hands with them both.

Evidently they were not the kind of people who would automatically embrace and kiss a stranger, even the wife of their son. Nicole liked them the better for it. She had never been comfortable with gushing in any form. It was one of the things she most disliked about Rosemary who left lipstick smears on the cheeks of all and sundry while being far from loving when at home.

The Strathallen's car was a large old-fashioned Bentley. 'You sit with me, Nicole,' he said, putting her into the front passenger seat.

In Nicole's world, men usually sat in front with women in the back to enable them to chat about matters of interest to their sex. She felt it would have been easier to make conversation with her mother-in-law than with this formidable chieftain, head of a branch of one of Scotland's ancient clans.

However, she needn't have worried. The Strathallen did most of the talking, pointing out features of the countryside they were passing through and reminiscing about his travels when younger.

They had been driving for an hour and she was feeling fairly relaxed when Strathallen, the house, came into view and revived her apprehensions. More castle than house, it was far larger and more imposing than Alex had led her to believe, with a pair of towers topped by turrets flanking the main entrance.

To Dan's delight, he was given the room in one of the towers where Alex had slept as a boy. No sooner had they unpacked than it was time for lunch. Afterwards, while his parents were busy with other things, Alex took them on a tour of the house and its grounds. Dan was impressed to discover that, in its oldest part, the building had a bottle dungeon where, long ago, prisoners had been forced to spend their imprisonment in an upright position.

To Nicole the dungeon was a grim reminder of a barbaric past. She was more interested in the many examples of fine needlework made by Strathallen wives and daughters, ranging from chair covers to the curtains on four-poster beds.

While they were in the gardens, the clear sky had clouded over and soon it began to rain, an unwelcome reminder that this was an inclement climate for much of the year. Soon the winter dusk drew in.

Nicole was relieved to find that, although parts of the house were not heated, the bathroom adjoining their bedroom was comfortably warm. Leaving Alex with Dan in her son's room, she decided to have a long bath before it was time to rejoin her in-laws.

In another part of the house, The Strathallen was asking his wife, 'Well…what do you think of her?'

He had just entered their bedroom, not having had a chance to talk to her privately since they returned from the airport.

'I'm puzzled…not just by Nicole…by both of them,' she said slowly. 'I like the look of her. Do you?'

'Yes…very good legs…dresses well…not too much make-up. Seems intelligent too. Why are you puzzled?'

'By the rather odd way they look at each other. Several times during lunch I saw her looking at him and Alex looking at her, but it wasn't the way newly-weds usually gaze at each other.'

'Would you expect that at their age? They're not in their twenties.'

'My dear, love is love at any age. There is something—' she searched for the right word '—something *guarded* about her. It's not only that she is nervous. Everyone is…meeting their in-laws for the first time. It goes deeper than that, I think.'

'You're always picking up signs that I haven't noticed,' her husband said, with an affectionate grin.

'Men never do notice nuances. You probably wouldn't have spotted a note being passed across the table. You only register what you're eating…and nice legs,' she added, with a twinkle. 'Seriously, Ian, I wasn't imagining it. They are neither of them quite relaxed. I might be imagining it with her, but not with Alex. I know him too well. There's something on his mind, I'm sure of it.'

'If there is, it's their business, not ours. I like the boy.'

'Yes, Dan is a darling. Very good manners and a sense of humour. Not in the least bit brattish which is a relief. I thought, being a single mother, she might not have had the time to bring him up properly. I'm not sure I could have coped on my own. I do hope—' She stopped short, frowning.

'You hope what?' he prompted quietly. A down-to-earth man with outsiders, her husband was far from insensitive. He knew she was too sensible to make mountains out of molehills. If she felt uneasy about their son's marriage, her intuition was likely to be right.

'I hope Alex hasn't married her on the strength of a chivalrous impulse. It can't have been easy for her and, now more than ever, her son needs a man to guide him. You know Alex always felt he was to blame for what happened to Nuala. I hope he hasn't married Nicole as some kind of…restitution.'

'I shouldn't think so for a moment,' her husband said

briskly. 'She isn't some poor plain Jane hardly able to make ends meet. She's a damned attractive girl and extremely talented.'

'I know, but there's still something vulnerable about her and Alex has always had strong protective instincts. He inherits them from you,' she added fondly.

'I don't know about that, but I do know he has more sense than to take on a long-term commitment impulsively,' said his father. 'Having seen the divorce figures soar among his contemporaries, he will have thought long and hard before marrying Nicole. The fact that, as she said at lunch, she took to India like a duck to water will have endeared her to him. She wouldn't have stood a chance with him if she hadn't shared that enthusiasm.'

'I'm very glad that she does, but I think love should be unconditional. It would worry me if I thought they didn't feel the same way.'

'Alex felt like that about Nuala,' her husband reminded her. 'You were worried about them.'

'Because they were so young. I don't think anyone is ready for marriage at that age. Would it have turned out well? We shall never know.' She sighed. 'I do so want him to be happy. He's been on his own far too long. Sharing one's life, with the right person, is so much better than being single.'

'I agree with you there, my love.' On his way to the adjoining bathroom, he paused to pat her shoulder. 'You have enough on your plate without worrying about your son and your new daughter-in-law. We shan't have them here for long. Why not enjoy it…let the future take care of itself?'

'You're right. I should and I will.'

But when he had gone for his bath, Mary Strathallen

could not help letting her mind dwell on whatever it was that made her vaguely uneasy about the second marriage she had been hoping would happen since her son turned thirty.

Now her dearest wish had been realised but her intuition told her that something was not as it should be. Perhaps, if there was an opportunity to get Alex on his own, or to have a private talk to Nicole, she might get to the bottom of it.

That evening, after dinner, while leading the way to the library where they had had drinks earlier, Nicole's mother-in-law said to her, 'My second daughter, Jenny, is mad about ballet. She's sent me a tape of something she saw on TV which she says we must watch. I thought we might see it this evening. Do you like ballet?'

'Yes, I do…not that I've seen much,' said Nicole.

Presently, while the grown-ups were drinking coffee, Mary Strathallen told the others her plan for their entertainment.

'Oh, Lord! Men in tights,' said her husband, rolling his eyes at Alex who was sharing the sofa with Nicole.

'You'll nod off anyway, Ian.' His wife inserted the video in the recorder and went back to her chair to press the necessary buttons. 'This is called *Zizi, Je T'aime*…Zizi, I Love You. It's about a famous dancer, Zizi Jeanmaire, and her husband Roland Petit, one of the world's great choreographers,' she told Dan, who was sitting near her, drinking cola. 'They met when they were nine years old and starting as pupils at the Paris Opera ballet school. When this film was made they were seventy-four but still astonishingly fit.'

Nicole wondered if he would be bored. He had been

on his best behaviour for hours and was probably longing to escape to his room and spend an hour on the
Net. She was looking forward to bedtime herself.
Despite her in-laws' friendliness, the day had been a
strain for her too.

The film included a clip from the ballet *Carmen*
which, overnight, had made international stars of Petit
and his beautiful ballerina and brought them offers
from Hollywood.

In the closing moments of the film, they danced together, as if on the floor of a nightclub. Although she
was wearing high heels, Zizi, her hair still cut close to
her shapely head in the way that emphasised her elfin
features, looked tiny compared with her husband.

The way he was looking down at her, clearly still as
enchanted by her as he had been half a century earlier,
made Nicole's throat constrict, her vision blur. If only
Alex felt that way about her.

'What did you think of it, Dan?' Mary Strathallen
asked him, as the credit titles started to roll.

'It was interesting,' he said politely.

'Perhaps you'd like to go up and read in bed now?'

'Oh, yes, please.' The way he jumped at the suggestion made the others laugh.

'I think we'll all turn in, Mum,' Alex said, rising.

He held his hand out to Nicole, a gesture she felt
was more for his mother's benefit than because he
wanted to touch her. Apart from the ordinary courtesies, outside the privacy of their bedroom he was spar-
ing with affectionate gestures.

Even in private he never kissed or caressed her except as foreplay. She had nothing to complain of in
regard to his lovemaking. It wasn't deteriorating into a
routine. But she wished he would be more affectionate

when they weren't making love. The small spontaneous gestures were what she longed for, but they weren't happening.

Sometimes, in the dark, he kissed her as if he wanted to devour her. But in public he might have been her brother rather than her husband.

She gave him her hand and let him pull her to her feet from the depths of the sofa. Expecting that to be the extent of the contact, she was surprised when he kept her fingers in his.

'Is breakfast still at a quarter to eight, Dad?'

'It is. I hope you sleep well, my dear.' This to Nicole.

'Thank you. I'm sure I shall.'

A few minutes later as they mounted the staircase with Dan running on ahead, Alex said, close to her ear, 'I shall make sure you sleep well.' He was still holding her hand. As he spoke, the tips of his fingers caressed the back of her palm.

'What are these, Alex?' On the landing, Dan was peering into a flat-topped glass case.

'A collection of fossils made by some long-dead Strathallen. There's a beetle trapped in amber. He was walking up the trunk of a tree when a trickle of resin or sap ran down and engulfed him. If you're interested, look at them tomorrow.'

'Can I pick up my email?'

He was asking Alex's permission rather than Nicole's and it pleased her that he accepted his stepfather's authority without the hostility she knew could occur, particularly among teenage boys who resented being told what to do by their mother's new husband or boyfriend. At least that wasn't a problem. Dan had looked up to Alex from day one.

'Sure, but only check your mail. Don't stay online. My father might want to use the phone. If you want to surf, do it first thing tomorrow. Nobody makes any calls before breakfast.'

They saw him as far as his door where Nicole kissed him goodnight and Alex brushed his cheek with his fist, a gesture Dan seemed to like.

On the way to their room, Alex recaptured her hand. 'Today hasn't been too bad, has it?'

'Your parents have been very nice. But it is rather awesomely grand compared with my background.'

'Backgrounds don't count any more. It's what people are like that matters.'

He opened their bedroom door for her, closed it behind him and, leaning against it, pulled her against him. 'I've been wanting you in my arms since that sexy scene in *Carmen* where he caught her in mid-air and she slid slowly down his body.'

The scene had excited her too. She had felt a shiver of longing to be as close as that to Alex. Now she was.

Sliding her arms round his neck, she whispered, 'I want you too.'

At least she could admit to desiring him, if not to loving him.

From Scotland they flew to London where Alex rented a car and drove them to the meeting that, in a different way, Nicole dreaded even more than her first encounter with her in-laws. She knew Alex would like her father, but what would he make of Rosemary?

When they drew up outside the house which for so long had been 'home' to her, it seemed to have shrunk in the months she had been away. The whole avenue of neat semi-detacheds with their cherry trees and laburnums and their aura of middle-class respectability had seemed dull to her when she lived here. Now she had been away, she understood her restlessness better. There were people who could be happy here, but she had known in her bones that she didn't belong in this environment. The place she would miss when they had to leave it would be Karangarh.

They stayed at her father's house for the few remaining days of Dan's holiday, after which Alex suggested they had some days by themselves in a comfortable country hotel before returning to London for the final week of their trip to Europe.

Dan wasn't too unhappy about going back to school. He was looking forward to telling his friends about his adventures in Rajasthan.

Strangely, Nicole found saying goodbye even more painful than the last time. Then she had also been venturing into the unknown. Now her future was clearly mapped and even if her marriage was flawed it was a better relationship than she had expected to come her way. But she wasn't totally comfortable about leaving her son.

When she talked about this to Alex, while he was driving a hired car to their country retreat, he said, 'That's just a maternal reflex. In a few years' time Dan will be leaving home altogether. He'll find it a lot easier for having already had some experience outside the nest. Late teenagers who've never had to fend for themselves can find it a hard transition. Even going to college is traumatic for some of them.'

'I suppose you're right. But last night, when I was in his room, I had the feeling there was something on his mind...that perhaps he wasn't looking forward to going back as much as he claimed.'

'I expect he was suffering from last-night-at-home syndrome. I always did. It's normal. Don't worry about it.'

The hotel Alex had chosen was a converted Elizabethan manor house combining character with modern comforts.

They unpacked, had a shower together, went to bed for a couple of hours and then went down to eat in a restaurant where, apart from one party of six, most of their fellow diners were in couples. The noise level was low, the service attentive, the atmosphere relaxing.

'What a long time it seems since our first meal together,' said Nicole, remembering how tense she had been on that occasion.

Tuning in to her thoughts, Alex smiled at her. 'You are more relaxed now.'

'Naturally...I know you better.'

'You could say that.' She could tell he was thinking about their time in bed.

In that sphere at least they were in perfect harmony: enjoying each other's bodies without restraint.

They made love again after dinner and, next morning, he woke her with kisses. Nicole liked touching his unshaven face. She found the slight roughness excitingly male, especially against the tender skin of her thighs. The more often they made love, the more rapidly she was aroused to the point where she had to grab a pillow and hold it over her face to muffle her cries of pleasure.

But later, after she had made love to him and then their bodies had fused for the final shared ecstasy, then came the let-down. Although, physically, she was satisfied, emotionally there was a shortfall. She needed to hear those three vital words—*I love you*.

* * *

After a leisurely breakfast they went for a long country walk, returning in time for lunch. Afterwards, in the comfortable drawing room made cosier by a log fire, Alex read the papers and Nicole enjoyed a browse through various glossy magazines.

'I think I'll go up and wash my hair,' she said presently.

'They serve afternoon tea at four,' he reminded her. 'Hot crumpets and home-made cakes.'

'I know, but do I need them? You stay and enjoy them. I'll see you later.'

She was halfway up the wide staircase when Alex caught her up. 'I'm going to pass on the crumpets.' There was no one about. He slid his arm round her waist. 'All I need more of is you. You can wash your hair later.'

In their room, he drew her against him as if it were days, not hours, since their last lovemaking. Nicole responded eagerly, closing her mind to the thought that passion, without love, was famous for burning out.

They had undressed each other and were in bed, kissing, when their privacy was disturbed.

'What the hell...?' Alex raised his head and glowered at the telephone. Then, reluctantly, he reached for the receiver. 'Yes?' he said curtly.

Wondering if the hotel switchboard had routed a call to the wrong room, Nicole waited for the interruption to end. After about half a minute she realised that Alex had been listening to the caller for too long for the call not to be for him. Also his frown had not lightened. His eyebrows were still drawn together. His lips which, moments before, had been gently teasing hers were now compressed in a way that indicated what he was hearing didn't please him.

So far he had said nothing, only listened and scribbled something on the notepad. Eventually he said briskly, 'I'll get back to you as soon as possible.'

Replacing the receiver, he rolled into a sitting position on the edge of the bed. It was clear before he spoke that they were not going to continue making love. Reaching for both her hands, holding them firmly in his, he said, 'That was Dan's headmaster. Dan has gone walkabout. He left a written note for the head. It refers to an email to you explaining why and where he's gone. In the note to Browning he only said the reason was private.'

'Oh, God…oh Dan…'

In the first moments of shock, all the horrifying news stories she had ever read swept through Nicole's mind like a flock of vultures. The thought of her son on his own in a world full of crackpots and criminals triggered a panic she found it hard to control.

Alex said quietly, 'Let's get your laptop plugged in. Where did you put it?'

'It's still in my case.' She sprang off the bed and rushed to the suitcase she hadn't fully unpacked yet. 'But what if there isn't an outlet I can plug into?'

'Then we'll take it downstairs to the manager's office. There'll be somewhere where it will work.'

His calmness stopped her from falling apart. Mercifully the hotel had made provisions for the type of guests known as 'road warriors', meaning business people who needed to be in constant touch with their headquarters and customers by email and the Internet.

Because her hands were unsteady, it was Alex who plugged the machine in and switched it on. Her fingers feeling all thumbs, Nicole keyed in her password and waited for the system to boot up. It seemed for ever

before she was able to click on 'Dan to Mum' and read
the message her son had left in her Inbox.

*Dear Mum, While we were visiting Granpa I
found out who my father is. I know you don't want
to have anything to do with him, but I'd like to meet
him, just once. I can't help being curious about him.
As he's famous, it's not going to be difficult to find
him. There are some fanzines about him on the Net.
He looks OK. Perhaps he's changed since you knew
him. Please don't worry about me. I'm old enough
to look after myself now. I'm not taking my laptop.
It's heavy to lug around and might get pinched. So
I can't keep in touch. But I'll be all right. If I haven't
found him in a few days, I'll come back. Love to you
and Alex. Dan xxxxx*

Alex had been looking over her shoulder at the
words on the screen. He said, 'He must have emailed
that just before he left. He'll be halfway to London by
now. What the headmaster wants to know is whether
to call in the police. At this stage, I think not. Once
the police are involved, the press will get hold of it.
That's the last thing you want…your private life plas-
tered all over the tabloids.'

'But the police are our only hope of finding him!'
she exclaimed. 'How would the press find out if we
wanted it kept strictly private?'

'Because the police are human beings,' he said
dryly. 'In most if not all police stations there's someone
who tips off the local press when anything newsworthy
comes up. The local reporters tip off the national press.
Anyway Dan is right: he *is* old enough to look after
himself. England isn't the dungheap of crime and vice

that the tabloid papers present it as. Good people still outnumber bad people by a high percentage.'

'Outside big cities, perhaps. But London is full of predators just waiting to prey on youngsters who arrive there on their own. You know it is.'

'You're thinking of children who have run away from home and want never to go back...children without any money or means of support. I'm sure Dan has adequate funds to carry out his plan. He'll have made a plan, you can bet on it. He's a sensible guy.'

'But he's only thirteen!' she wailed. 'Where is he going to spend the night? A hotel wouldn't give him a room, nor would a youth hostel. He's tall for his age, but he couldn't pass for sixteen.'

'Have a look at these fanzines he's mentioned and see if they give a clue to where he might find his father,' Alex advised. 'I don't think they will, but Dan has to have something to go on. He wouldn't have taken off without some sort of lead.'

Forcing herself to concentrate, Nicole did a search on the Internet and found several websites devoted to the man who was the cause of this crisis. Two sites were the work of fans but the third was part of a big commercial website funded by one of the big recording companies. None of the sites gave any indication of where in London Pete lived. She hadn't expected them to. The last thing any pop star wanted was to have his privacy invaded by a horde of excited groupies.

'We'd better call Browning back...will you talk to him?' Alex asked.

She nodded. 'Are you *sure* we shouldn't call the police?'

'Definitely not tonight. We need time to think this thing through.'

But it was tonight that worried her. In daylight her son was less at risk. But at night, sleeping out in the open—and she couldn't see any alternative to that—a young boy was frighteningly vulnerable to thieves and other molesters. At the same time she felt that Alex was a better judge of the situation than she was. She knew that he cared about Dan and would protect him with his life if the necessity arose. He might never come to love her, but his affection for her son was evident every time they were together.

The headmaster, when she spoke to him, did not try to persuade her to change her mind about the police. Nor did he press her for the reason for Dan's absence. Perhaps he sensed that a damaging scandal was looming over his school and, although deeply concerned for Dan's safety, was equally concerned about the effect on the school and other parents if a pack of press and TV reporters descended on it.

'Please keep in close touch, Ms Dawson,' he said, at the end of their conversation.

Nicole promised she would and put the phone down. Throughout the call Alex had been pacing the room. She felt sure he had registered everything she had said, but she sensed that his mind had also been working on something else.

Now he stopped pacing and looked at her. 'That bank account you told me about…the fund Dan's father started for him. What bank and what branch? Do you have the details with you?'

'They're on my hard disk in a file I transfer every time I upgrade my machine.'

'Look them up, will you?'

It was a matter of moments to locate the file and open it,

Alex made some more notes on the jotting pad. 'If we can't make contact with Dan, we can at least try to contact his father.'

'How? The bank won't reveal his whereabouts. They might forward a letter to him, but that could take ages.'

'No information is sacrosanct if you know the right person to ask. One of my brothers-in-law is in banking. He will know. Close down your notebook and I'll call him.'

When, within seconds of dialling the number, he began dictating a message, her heart sank. His brother-in-law might only be out for the evening, or he might be away on a trip. Anyway tracking down Pete wasn't really going to help. It was Dan they had to find before something terrible happened to him.

'I'm sure this isn't an impulse thing. He's been planning it for some time,' she said, speaking her thoughts aloud. 'I should have known there was something on his mind. If I hadn't been preoccupied with other things...I blame myself for not noticing he was unhappy.'

'What makes you think he was unhappy?'

'If he was happy, he wouldn't have run away.'

'I don't think he has run away. His curiosity about his natural father has become too strong to resist. It was bound to happen sooner or later.'

'Nobody ever really knows what's going on inside other people. Perhaps he's felt...excluded. All his life he's had me to himself. Deep down he may not like having to share me.'

Alex came to where she was sitting and sat beside her, putting his arm round her shoulders. 'Dan isn't the kind of over-indulged, self-centred child who would feel that. He's in no doubt about how much you love him…and he adores you.'

There was something in the way he said it that made her think, just for a fraction of a second, that it might be Alex himself who felt excluded from her bond with her son. But a moment later she recognised the thought as merely wishful thinking, to which she had always been prone and more so since meeting him.

'He may find our marriage disturbing,' she said. 'Adolescent boys have problems adjusting to their own sexuality. They're uncomfortable with the idea of their parents having a sex life, especially their mothers.'

'I've been a teenage boy. Believe me, they don't have half the hang-ups that psychiatrists and other do-gooders would like to pin on them. I doubt if Dan's given a thought to what you and I do in private.'

'Your parents had always been married. It's different for the children of single parents. They're a lot less secure…a lot more easily upset.'

'That depends on their temperament,' Alex told her. 'I've spent enough time with Dan to know that he's as solid as they come.'

'But if he was desperate to meet his father, why didn't he tell me?'

'He probably thought you wouldn't agree to a meeting. It was better to go ahead and do it, without involving you. You had better let your father know where we are. In your absence, he's the person Dan will call if he decides to make contact. There's no need to worry your father by telling him what's happened. Just give him the name and number of the hotel so that, if necessary, he can call us.'

When the time came for dinner, Nicole knew she couldn't eat a full meal and Alex agreed that he wasn't hungry either. He rang Room Service to order sandwiches, a pot of coffee and a bottle of wine.

At ten o'clock he ran a bath for her. 'You must try to get some sleep. A warm bath will help.'

After her bath, he insisted she had some hot chocolate laced with brandy as another aid to sleep.

Surprisingly, she did sleep through part of that long night. Having Alex curled round behind her made her feel less distraught than had she been on her own.

Several long wakeful periods caused her to oversleep the following morning. Alex was already dressed when she opened her eyes and found him sitting in a chair he had moved close to her side of the bed.

'You should have woken me,' she protested, seeing what time it was.

'You needed more rest. We'll have breakfast, then drive to London. If that's where his father lives when he's not on tour, that's where Dan will show up. We can use Kesri's flat.'

CHAPTER NINE

WHEN they arrived at the flat, Jal said to Nicole, 'I have a telephone message for you, madam…an urgent message. A gentleman would like you to call him back at your earliest convenience. I've written his name and number by the telephone in the drawing room.' He opened the door for her.

Nicole thanked him and hurried to the telephone on an end table by one of the sofas where she and Alex had sat when he'd interviewed her. On the pad, in Jal's neat hand, was written *Pete Jones* and a number starting with the outer London code.

'It's Dan's father,' she told Alex, starting to dial.

Her call was answered by a man with a foreign accent. She gave her name and told him about the message.

'Hold the line, please. I will ask.'

In a fever of impatience, she waited for what seemed a long time. With her hand over the mouthpiece, she said, 'He must know something. Why else would he have called?'

Before Alex could answer, a voice she hadn't heard for almost fourteen years said, 'Hi, Nicky. You can stop worrying. He's here.'

'Thank God!' For the first time in her life Nicole felt as if she might faint. The relief of knowing Dan was safe made her eyes brim with tears, her lips quiver. She sank onto the sofa, starting to shake with reaction to the hours of being tense with anxiety.

'He's safe...he's all right,' she told Alex. Then, speaking to Pete, 'How did he find you? How long has he been with you?'

'Not long...a couple of hours. We could have touched base sooner if you'd had a mobile. Dan says you don't like them.'

She had once read in a magazine that, when missing children were restored to them, parents were often more angry than joyful. Now she learned this for herself. If Dan had been in the room, she would have had difficulty controlling the urge to shake him until his teeth rattled.

'Is he there? I want to speak to him.'

She heard Pete say, 'Your mum wants a word.'

Then a nervous voice said, 'I'm sorry if you were worried.'

'Not half as sorry as you're going to be! How could you? How *could* you be so totally irresponsible? I thought you had more sense. I thought I could trust you...rely on you. Have you any idea what you've put us through, you thoughtless, selfish little beast?'

Her rage poured out in a flood of angry upbraidings that came to an abrupt end when her voice cracked and she burst into tears.

As, still holding the phone to her ear, she wiped them away with her free hand, Dan said in a quavery voice, 'Please don't cry, Mum...I'm sorry...I'm sorry.' He was starting to cry himself. Sniffs and gulps could be heard down the line.

Then, as her anger evaporated and she wanted to hug him, the phone was taken away from her and replaced by a man-sized handkerchief.

'Dan, this is Alex. I want to speak to your father.'

Overwhelmed by emotion, Nicole heard Alex's side

of the conversation with Pete without making any sense of it. She was still in floods when it ended and her husband took her in his arms, holding her head against his shoulder and stroking and patting her back, as she would have comforted her child had he been there.

When the outburst finally stopped and she could speak coherently, she said, in a husky murmur, 'I don't make a habit of this. I haven't cried for years.'

'There are extenuating circumstances.' Alex tipped up her face and smoothed her hair from her forehead and temples.

The caress was infinitely tender. It made her remember what she had seen before but been too distracted to think about: the look in his eyes when she'd told him that Dan was safe. Not just a look of relief, but something more. Now, thinking about it, she was almost prepared to swear that what had been there was the very same expression she remembered seeing in her father's eyes when she was a little girl and he was looking at her mother.

Alex, do you love me? The question hovered at the tip of her tongue. Afraid to say it aloud, in case she had made a mistake, she asked, 'What happens next? Are we going to fetch him?'

'His father will bring him to us. But not till this evening. He wants Dan to spend the day there. I think that's a good idea. It will give you a breathing space to recover from the bad time you've been through. It will give them a chance to talk. They need to talk, Nicole. Pete is a rat to have walked out as he did. But it doesn't alter the fact that he's the boy's father.'

'Only his biological father. That's not much of a link with nothing to back it up. I don't want Dan to be dazzled by the pop star image. He's not old enough to discriminate between the image and the reality. If Pete hadn't been a star, would he have gone in search of him?'

'My guess is that he would. Why do people spend time and money tracing their forebears? Why do third-generation Americans want to visit the places where their grandparents were born? Why are adopted children curious about their natural parents? It's all part of the search for identity.' He rose from the sofa. 'What you need is a cup of tea.'

'And to wash my face?' said Nicole. 'Is it all right to use the bathroom we had when we stayed here?'

'Of course.'

When she returned, looking less of a wreck, the tea tray was already on the low table.

'I've telephoned the school and told them that all is well,' said Alex, as she crossed the room.

'Oh, my goodness, I'd forgotten about the school. Who did you speak to?'

'The head's secretary. I didn't go into details, just said Dan was safe and well and we'd bring him back in a few days' time.'

'Thank you, Alex. Thank you for everything. You've been a rock through all this. If you hadn't been with me last night, I'd have fallen apart.'

He began to pour out the tea. 'You're not the falling apart type. You held up very well. I can guess how frantic you must have been feeling inside.'

'Not nearly as frantic as if I'd been on my own.'

She saw his face harden with anger. 'Mothers are notoriously soft touches. You will probably go easy on him. But I shall have something more forceful to say to him. He put you through hell and he needs to be made to realise that.'

'I'm sure he does realise already. He was crying when you took the phone from me. Don't be too hard on him, Alex. You said yourself that wanting to find Pete was natural.'

'Yes, but frightening his mother was an asinine thing to do. He should have been open about it…though look who's talking,' he added.

Puzzled by his tone, she asked, 'What do you mean?'

Alex drained his cup and put it back on the table. Leaning forward, his wrists on his knees, he interlaced his long fingers and looked at them, not at her.

'I haven't been straight with you, Nicole. I've been concealing something. Perhaps this isn't the moment to get it off my chest, but every day I find it harder to live with.'

She felt ice forming round her heart. Was he going to tell her their marriage had been a mistake? Surely not now…not on top of another bad shock?

'What is it? Tell me.' She clenched her right hand and wrapped her other hand round it, bracing herself not to show pain.

Alex straightened and turned to face her. 'The first time we sat in this room I fell in love with you…but I didn't recognise the feeling for what it was. Also, because of what happened to Nuala, my first wife, I didn't want to expose myself in that way. I resisted it as long as possible. Now I can't keep it in any longer. I have to tell you how I feel.'

In a different way, it was as much of a shock as the confession she had been praying not to hear.

'But you said…I thought…' She floundered.

'I said a lot of stupid things that seemed sensible at the time. I thought if I told you the truth it might put you off. Love, when it isn't mutual, can be a burden.

Nobody likes being under an obligation, especially when what is required of them isn't possible.'

'But it is…oh, Alex, *it is*!' she exclaimed. 'I fell in love with you too. I could hardly bear bottling it up…never being able to say the words in my heart.'

She reached out her hands and he took them in his strong clasp. In his eyes was the same expression she had glimpsed before, but this time quite unmistakable.

'I did sometimes think you might be beginning to feel more warmly towards me.'

'Not *warmly*…that sounds far too tepid. I wanted your love so much I felt like a human volcano in constant danger of erupting.'

'That's rather the way I felt. I could only express my feelings by making love to you. But that's only part of love. There is so much more to it and all the rest seemed off limits.' He paused, looking into her eyes. 'But nothing is off limits now…my dearest darling.'

He said the last words with a relish she understood, having so often longed to use endearments to him.

Then he drew her closer and framed her face with his hands. 'Let's go to bed. I'll tell Jal we had a bad night and need to catch up on our sleep. He probably won't believe me, but it will give him a reason not to disturb us if anyone calls.'

When Nicole woke, she could hear taps running in the adjoining bathroom. She was lazily stretching her arms and legs, filled with a deep sense of well-being, when Alex appeared, a towel wrapped round his lean hips.

'I've run you a bath. They're due to arrive around six. Jones can park his car in the basement. Not all the residents have cars so there's always room for visitors to park.'

As he spoke he drew back the duvet and, scooping her up in his arms, carried her to the bathroom where he set her down in front of the long mirror. Standing behind her, he ran his hands possessively down her sides. They smiled at each other's reflection. It had always been good but this afternoon had been better because they were no longer hiding things from each other.

'I'll leave you to have a relaxing soak.' He gave her a pat on the behind and went back to the bedroom.

Nicole stepped into the water and sank down into its scented warmth. But it wasn't possible to relax completely until the meeting with Pete was over. She wondered how much he had changed. She had always avoided looking at shop displays that might include the sleeves of his records and CDs, and quickly turned the pages of papers and magazines dealing with pop musicians.

She wondered if he would want to see his son again and couldn't help hoping he wouldn't. She didn't want Dan getting involved with the meretricious world of showbiz. But had she the right to intervene if they both wanted to see more of each other?

Later, when she asked Alex what he thought, he said, 'Don't cross your bridges before you come to them, angel. Would a drink help to steady the nerves?'

'Yes, please. I do feel rather jittery. How did you guess?'

'It would be strange if you weren't.' He dropped ice into two tall glasses, poured generous measures of gin topped up with tonic and added thin slices of lemon.

He carried the drinks to where she was standing.
'Here's to us and the future.'

She echoed the toast and drank, feeling the kick of
the spirit, hoping it would take the edge off her appre-
hension.

Moments later they heard the bell ring, starting a
flutter of butterflies in her stomach. As she turned to
face the door, Alex moved closer, stationing himself at
her side.

It wasn't Jal who opened the door. It was Dan. He
hovered on the threshold. 'Are you still angry, Mum?'

Nicole had already put down her drink. Now, smil-
ing, she shook her head and opened her arms to him.
He came charging across the room. If she hadn't been
braced for the impact, he could have knocked her over.
She was still being bear-hugged when Jal appeared.
'Your visitors, madam.' He ushered them in.

If Nicole had passed him in the street, she might not
have recognised Pete. Maturity and success had
changed the youth who had been her lover into a different person from the one she remembered. With him
was a head-turning redhead in black leather trousers
and an expensive fake fur jacket thrown open to show
a bosom-hugging black turtle-necked body.

It was Alex who reacted first. Stepping forward, he
offered his hand to the redhead. 'Good evening. I'm
Alex Strathallen…Nicole's husband.'

'Hi, Alex. Pleased to meet you. I'm Suzi…Pete's
girlfriend.'

Alex did not offer his hand to Pete, Nicole noticed.
He confined himself to saying good evening and asking
them if they would like a drink.

'Nice place you've got here,' Pete said to Nicole,
looking round the elegant room.

'It isn't ours. One of Alex's friends allows us to use it.'

'Dad's got a fab house, Mum. It's got a big indoor pool as well as one in the garden.'

'How did you find out where he lived?' she asked her son.

'I went to the public library. They helped me to look up the name and address of his agent. I went to the agent's office and asked them to ask Dad if I could come and see him.'

Pete said, 'I thought he might show up one day so I left instructions that if ever a kid called Daniel asked for me, they were to let me know straight away. It was clever of him to get to them.'

'It wasn't clever to give his mother a sleepless night,' Alex intervened coldly. After handing them their drinks, he said, 'I want a word with you, Dan.' He beckoned the boy to follow him out of the room.

After the door closed behind them, there was an awkward silence until Pete said, 'You haven't been married long, then?'

'Not very long, no. I've been concentrating on my career…and on bringing up Dan.' In case that sounded resentful, which wasn't the impression she wanted to give, she went on, 'Has he told you about his visit to India?'

'He never stopped talking about it,' Suzi said, with a laugh. 'The palace…the desert…Prince Whatshisname. The kid's crazy about it. I don't think I'd want to go there. I don't like places with snakes.' She gave a dramatic shudder.

'We didn't see any snakes,' said Nicole. She turned to Peter. 'I'm sorry if Dan turning up unexpectedly was inconvenient for you. Alex feels that it's natural for him to be curious, especially when he learned you were a pop star. I hadn't mentioned that to him. Someone else told him. I don't know who it was. Did he tell you?'

'Some kid he met somewhere while you were staying with your dad,' Pete told her, with a shrug.

'It's a wonder he didn't find out sooner...seeing his dad's a celeb,' said Suzi. 'He's a sweet little fella, Nicky. Lovely manners compared with some I could mention. My sister's a single mother, but she's divorced. My nephews have really run wild since their old man walked out. You've done a great job on Danny.'

'Thank you,' Nicole said politely, inwardly seething at Suzi's familiarity and the hint of patronage underlying her chummy manner.

She was also concerned about what might be happening elsewhere in the apartment. She felt it would have been better for Alex to have postponed reading the riot act until tomorrow. She hoped he wouldn't be *too* hard on Dan and damage the good relationship they had had until now.

'So are you going back to India?' Pete asked.

'For the foreseeable future. As Dan may have told you, Alex is an anthropologist.' Seeing that Suzi was looking puzzled, she explained what he did.

'Dan doesn't seem all that keen on this boarding-school you're sending him to,' said Pete. 'He could come to us for the half-term holiday and the exits. We could give him a better time than he'd have with your dad and his wife. She sounds a proper old dragon.'

Nicole wasn't sure how to deal with this suggestion. Playing for time, she said, 'The school's short holidays are called exeats. It's Latin. It means ''he may go out''.

I think Dad would be upset if Dan didn't spend time with them, especially as he won't be seeing him in the long holidays. Dad's health isn't good. He's aged a lot since you knew him.'

'Gorblimey! An invalid grandad and a fussy step-granny...that's no fun at all for the poor kid,' said Suzi, putting her oar in. 'We could give him a really good time.'

Longing for Alex to come back, Nicole decided to be blunt. 'Why would you want to be lumbered with someone else's child?' she asked her.

Momentarily flummoxed, Suzi made a quick recovery. 'He wouldn't be no trouble. I don't have a lot else to do. All the cleaning and cooking is done by Maria and Diego and we have a driver and a gardener. I only have to keep Peter happy...and I do, don't I, gorgeous?' She nudged his arm with her elbow and gave a sexy giggle, making him grin and slip an arm round her shoulders.

By now Nicole was determined that Dan should not be exposed to the influence of a bird-brain like Suzi who would probably lavish him with presents and undo years of sensible training. She was about to say that she wouldn't dream of letting her son stay with strangers, which was what these two were, when Alex rejoined them.

'Dan has asked me to say goodnight and to thank you for having him,' he said to the other two. 'He didn't get much sleep last night so he's pretty worn out.' He turned to Nicole. 'He didn't fancy dossing down in a doorway in London. He broke his journey in the country, found a field and slept in a sleeping bag. Luckily it was a dry night. Then he caught a bus to Victoria coach station.'

'He didn't tell us that,' said Suzi. 'We had no idea he'd been out all night. He's got more guts than I have. I'd be scared to death, all on my own in a field in the dead of night.'

'I don't think Dan enjoyed it,' Alex said dryly.

'I was just saying to Nicky that it would be nice, while you're off in India, for him to spend time with us. Being parked with old people isn't much fun for a teenager, is it?'

Alex looked thoughtfully at her. 'I always had a wonderful time with my grandmother. Even in her eighties she was tremendously good company.' He turned to Nicole. 'It's up to you where Dan spends his exeats, but I think he should spend some time with your father and the rest in Scotland, getting to know my nephews and nieces.' He turned to the others. 'Nicole would probably be reluctant to say this, but the fact is that we don't know you or how you live. You and your friends may be the salt of the earth. But the pop music world isn't noted for its sobriety and morality. Dan is a little too young to cope with influences that might conflict with the way he's been raised by his mother.'

'What bloody cheek!' exclaimed Suzi. 'Are you suggesting that Pete and me are—?'

'Calm down, Suze,' Pete began.

Alex silenced them both by saying quietly, 'If, when he's older, Dan wants a closer relationship with his natural father, that's up to him. But by virtue of marrying Nicole, I'm his adoptive father and it's my intention to play a more active role in the rest of his childhood than you have so far.' He was looking at Pete as he spoke and it was clear to Nicole that he wasn't impressed by him.

Suzi would have flared up again, but Pete restrained

her with a hand on her arm, and a brusque, 'Shut it, will you? This is none of your business.'

Although she didn't like the other woman, Nicole couldn't help being shocked by the uncouth way he told her to be quiet. He had always been a rough diamond by her father's standards. Clearly he still was.

'Is that how you feel?' he asked Nicole.

'Yes, I'm afraid it is. If you had any real fatherly feelings you would have shown them before now. I think Dan's a novelty to you, but your interest will soon wear off. He's already had to come to terms with your absence from his life. If you were to make a fuss of him and then get bored and drop him, it could be very damaging.'

For a moment or two he was silent, staring at her with a brooding expression. Then he sprang to his feet. 'Right then, if that's your attitude, there's no more to be said. Come on, Suze. Let's not pollute the air these two high-minded people have to breathe any longer.'

He marched out of the room, leaving her to follow. Near the door, she looked back, her expression aggressive. 'I could tell you were a stuck-up bitch the minute I saw you.'

Nicole surprised herself. 'And I thought you looked a gold-digging tart,' she retorted.

Suzi opened her mouth, but before she could utter whatever screech of abuse she had in mind, Pete reappeared, grabbed her and hauled her out of sight.

Raising his eyebrows at Nicole, Alex crossed the room, either to close the door or perhaps, with Jal not attending to Peter and Suzi's departure, to see them off the premises.

But it seemed that the manservant's sharp ears had caught the sound of Suzi's unladylike language as Peter hustled her away. There was no slamming of the outer door as Nicole had expected. Jal must have materialised in time to prevent it. She heard Alex say, 'Thank you, Jal,' before he came back into the drawing room and she could let out her breath in a long gasp of relief.

'I shouldn't have answered her back,' she said apologetically, knowing that his mother would never have allowed herself to be goaded into an exchange of insults.

To her surprise, he laughed. 'I was tempted to say "Hear, hear". Would you like another drink?'

'Yes, please. That was quite an ordeal. What very bad taste in men I had at the age of eighteen.'

'What much better taste in women Dan's father had then than now,' Alex responded.

'What did you say to Dan after you took him away?'

'Most of it was a repeat of the dressing-down my father gave me after I frightened my mother by damn nearly breaking my neck.'

'What happened?'

'I was older than Dan. Sixteen. So there was less excuse for me. A friend and I went climbing. We thought we knew more than we did and I fell off the rock face and staggered home bleeding from a head wound. It looked worse than it was, as head injuries often do, but I had to be taken to hospital and X-rayed and kept in for observation for a couple of nights. My mother kept calm at the time, but she was upset. When I was allowed home, my father tore me to shreds. I did the same to Dan.'

'How did he take it?'

Alex finished refreshing their drinks and came to sit down beside her. 'He took it like his mother's son. It's obvious most of his genes come from you.'

'You didn't make him cry?'

'No, no, he wouldn't have cried if I'd hung him up by his thumbs. That's not to say he didn't have a quiet boohoo after I sent him to bed. We've all done that on occasion. But he certainly didn't cry while I was blasting him. The upper lip was so stiff it didn't even quiver.'

'Oh, dear, poor Dan,' murmured Nicole, her heart wrung by the thought of all that her son had been through in the past twenty-four hours. 'I hope he's not crying now. I think I ought to go and see.'

When she would have risen, Alex restrained her by looping his fingers round her wrist. 'He'll be having a bath. Drink your drink…give him time to recover. If he has been crying, he won't want you to know it. And don't worry: he won't resent my telling him off. He knows why I was angry. Because I love you…and him.'

'Do you really? Already?' She had thought it would take much longer for Alex to come to love Dan.

'How could I not when he's your son? And very like you.'

'Is he? People have said that, but I've never seen it. But nor do I think he's like his father. Pete was only here a short time, but I couldn't see any vestige of resemblance between them.'

'I might have liked Pete if I hadn't known what he'd done to you. But that girlfriend of his is a pain. If she ever has a child, it will be spoiled rotten one day and shouted and sworn at the next. You didn't mind what I said to her, I hope?'

'Of course not! While you were out of the room I asked her why she wanted to be bothered with him. What you told her was spot on. It would never surprise me if both of them had a drug habit. It's not unusual in showbiz circles. Even if they don't do drugs, I'm certain their outlook is completely different from ours. Suzi would probably buy Dan all sorts of flash clothes. She might even encourage him to wear a safety pin in his ear,' she added jokingly.

'Mr Browning would love that,' Alex said, smiling. 'What's your feeling about when to take Dan back to school? Shall we let him have a couple of days with us, calming down after all the excitement?'

'I certainly don't think we ought to hurry him back there tomorrow. Oh, Alex—' she put her hand on his leg '—you can't imagine how wonderful it is to have someone I can talk to about Dan. After Dad married Rosemary, it was virtually impossible ever to get him alone. So there was no one to share my problems with.'

He put a hand over hers. 'Even when there are no problems, it's good to have someone to share life's pleasures. I've told Jal that we'll dine *à deux* and Dan will have supper in bed. He should be out of the bath now if you want to check how he's doing.'

'I shan't be long,' she promised.

She found Dan already in bed, wearing a too-large T-shirt that Jal must have found for him.

'This is better than last night,' he said, as she sat on the bed. 'It was a bit scary being on my own after dark. I know it was a stupid thing to do, Mum. It's just that I've always wondered about him and when I found out who he was...' He paused, fidgeting with the edge of the duvet. 'Yesterday I was thinking about telling people at school that my dad was a pop star. But now that I've met him...' He paused.

'Did he disappoint you?' she asked. 'I thought you

were impressed by the two swimming pools and everything.'

'The pools were great but...I dunno...Pete isn't like Alex.' After another pause, he burst out, 'I wish Alex was my dad.'

'He's the next best thing, your stepfather,' Nicole said gently. 'Do you want to see Pete and Suzi again?'

Dan considered the question. 'Not really,' he said finally. 'They're OK but they're not like us. There's stuff in their house that you'd hate. Suzi thinks if it cost a lot it must be nice. She took me up to their bedroom. The bed was huge, all piled up with fancy lace pillows and dolls and furry animals, like a little girl's bed.'

'That might be because she didn't have anyone or anything to cuddle when she was little and she's making up for it now,' Nicole suggested. 'It would be a boring world if we all had identical bedrooms.'

There was a tap at the door and Jal entered, carrying a tray with short legs that he let down before placing it across the boy's lap.

'I will be serving dinner in five minutes, madam,' he said, in his quiet lilting voice.

'Thank you, Jal. I'm just coming.' She had already risen. When he had left the room, she lingered for a few moments, watching Dan start to eat.

'I'll look in again later on.'

'Can I read for a bit?' he asked. There was a stack of new books on the night table, as there was in all the bedrooms.

'For a bit, but not for too long. It's been a strenuous day. When you've finished your supper hop out and brush your teeth.'

His mouth full, Dan nodded.

*   *   *

Alex had been watching the news on TV, but he switched it off when she joined him. 'Unlike our small corner of it, the outside world has had a quiet day for a change. How's Dan bearing up?'

'He's tucking into his supper as if nothing had happened. But I'm sure everything you said to him has been taken on board and won't be forgotten in a hurry.'

'I wouldn't count on it,' Alex said, smiling. 'It's not in the nature of boys to stop and think before they act. That kind of prudence comes later. Though he did show a good deal of sense in preferring to sleep in a field than in a big city doorway. Except that, if it had rained, he'd have been a drowned rat by morning.'

For them, Jal's wife had prepared a more elaborate dinner than Dan's grilled halibut with chips. With their main dishes—lamb with rice and several kinds of vegetables—came a napkin-lined basket of *pooris*. Nicole thought these balloons of bread made by deep-frying discs of dough were, when eaten hot, the most delicious of all the many Indian breads.

The lamb had been cooked with cloves, cardamom and cinnamon. She was enjoying the distinctive blend of spices when she looked up from her plate and saw that Alex had stopped eating and was watching her.

Before she could ask what he was thinking, he told her. 'I'm still not used to the idea that, after a long time alone, I'm going to have your lovely face on the other side of the table "To-morrow, and to-morrow, and to-morrow".'

'Where does that come from?'

'Shakespeare...*Macbeth*. It's one of the few lines I remember.'

As always when he spoke of the future, she could not help being reminded that this special kind of happiness, which for her was a new thing, he had experienced before, only to have it snatched from him.

With disconcerting insight, he said, 'You're thinking about Nuala who lost her tomorrows.'

'Yes, I was,' she admitted. 'You must think of her sometimes…don't you?'

'We grew up together so, yes, I think of her sometimes, as I think of my sisters. But the short time we were together is like one of those dreams that, when morning comes, you can't remember properly.'

He leaned across the table to cover one of her hands with one of his. 'I thought I would have a problem being civil to Pete. I was as jealous as hell of what he had once meant to you. But when I met him today that feeling evaporated. He was merely a part of your past that had lost its importance. Who you were then—who I was—is not who we are today. It's only the future that matters…a future we're going to share.'

Not very long after dinner, they decided to go to bed. When, on the way to their room, they looked in on Dan, his reading lamp was on but he had fallen asleep. There was no sign of his supper tray so Jal must have taken it earlier.

Nicole removed the book Dan had been reading and stooped to kiss his cheek. Then she straightened, switched off the lamp and turned towards the tall figure standing in the doorway, silhouetted by the light from the passage.

She knew intuitively that, very soon, Alex was going to make love to her again. She thought of how far they had travelled, not only in air miles but in their hearts and souls, since the first time she came here.

It would have been so easy for them to miss each other and never find the happiness they had now. But, thanks to Kesri, they had made it to the safe haven of each other's arms.

Author's note: The city I have called Karangarh is a synthesis of several walled cities I visited in Rajasthan.

If you enjoyed what you just read,
then we've got an offer you can't resist!

Take 2 bestselling
love stories FREE!
Plus get a FREE surprise gift!

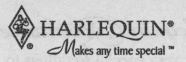

HARLEQUIN®
Makes any time special™

WIN A DREAM

In celebration of Harlequin®'s golden anniversary

Enter to win a *dream!* You could win:

- A luxurious trip for two to
  The Renaissance Cottonwoods Resort
  in Scottsdale, Arizona, or
- A bouquet of flowers once a week for a year
  from FTD, or
- A $500 shopping spree, or
- A fabulous bath & body gift basket, including
  K-tel's *Candlelight and Romance* 5-CD set.

Look for **WIN A DREAM** flash on
specially marked Harlequin® titles by
Penny Jordan, Dallas Schulze,
Anne Stuart and Kristine Rolofson
in October 1999*.

FTD

RENAISSANCE.
COTTONWOODS RESORT
SCOTTSDALE, ARIZONA

K·TEL

Harlequin Romance®

**brings you four very special weddings to
remember in our new series:**

WHITE WEDDINGS

True love is worth waiting for....

Look out for the following titles by some of
your favorite authors:

August 1999—SHOTGUN BRIDEGROOM #3564
Day Leclaire
Everyone is determined to protect Annie's good name and ensure
that bad boy Sam's seduction attempts don't end in the
bedroom—but begin with a wedding!

September 1999—A WEDDING WORTH WAITING FOR #3569
Jessica Steele
Karrie was smitten by boss Farne Maitland. But she was
determined to be a virgin bride. There was only one solution:
marry and quickly!

October 1999—MARRYING MR. RIGHT #3573
Carolyn Greene
Greg was wrongly arrested on his wedding night for something he
didn't do! Now he's about to reclaim his virgin bride when he dis-
covers Christina's intention to marry someone else....

November 1999—AN INNOCENT BRIDE #3577
Betty Neels
Katrina didn't know it yet but Simon Glenville, the wonderful doctor
who'd cared for her sick aunt, was in love with her. When the time
was right, he was going to propose....

Available wherever Harlequin books are sold.

HARLEQUIN®
Makes any time special.™

Look us up on-line at: http://www.romance.net

HRWW

♯Harlequin Romance®

Coming Next Month

#3575 BRIDEGROOM ON APPROVAL Day Leclaire
Hanna went to the Cinderella Ball intending to bring home a
husband—on a trial-only basis! Marco Salvatore wasn't looking for a
bride, yet he wanted Hanna the moment he saw her. They were married
by midnight...but could this marriage last a lifetime?

Fairytale Weddings: *The Fairytale Weddings Ball: come
single, leave wed!*

#3576 ONE MOTHER WANTED Jeanne Allan
Zane Peters, the man Allie once loved—still loves—needs a wife if he is
to keep custody of his motherless little girl. Allie offers to marry him for
his daughter's sake. But can she ever become his wife for real?

Hope Valley Brides: *Four weddings, one Colorado family*

#3577 AN INNOCENT BRIDE Betty Neels
Aunt Thirza's death had left Katrina with a small cottage—and, though
she didn't know it, Simon Glenville, the wonderful doctor who had
cared for her aunt. He knew he loved Katrina, and when the time was
right he would propose....

White Weddings: *True love is worth waiting for....*

#3578 OUTBACK WIFE AND MOTHER Barbara Hannay
Fletcher Hardy was adamant that his cattle station was no place for a
city-girl like Ally. Until she turned up at Wallaroo as his four-year-old
godson's new nanny, intending to prove she could survive the
Outback—and be the perfect wife and mother!

Daddy Boom: *Who says bachelors and babies don't mix?*